ASSASSIN'S HEART

Assassins 3

Ella Sheridan

Praise for *ASSASSINS*

"Entertaining, fast-paced, with twists and turns that will keep you on your toes. Seriously, my Kindle was smoking!" – Anna's Bookshelf

"My heart took a beating but taking a break — stop reading?? — was never an option. I started this story and didn't come up for air once." —1-Click Addict Support Group

"Full of intrigue, action, and some scorching chemistry between our favorite assassin and the ever fiesty Abby. There were moments when I gasped and struggled not to throw my kindle and other moments where I thought my kindle would spontaneously combust from the hot scenes between Levi and Abby. " — Anna's Bookshelf

"Holy hotness Batman, this book could leave scorch marks!" – GA Book LoverX

Ella Sheridan

Also by Ella Sheridan

Assassins

The Assassin

Assassin's Mark

Assassin's Prey

Assassin's Heart

Assassin's Game

Southern Nights

Teach Me

Trust Me

Take Me

Southern Nights: Enigma

Come for Me

Deceive Me

Destroy Me

Deny Me

If Only

Only for the Weekend

Only for the Night

Assassin's Heart

Only for the Moment

Secrets

Unavailable

Undisclosed

Unshakable

∞

Don't miss the exciting extras from the ASSASSINS series, available only through my newsletter. Sign up at my website, ellasheridanauthor.com, to get exclusive access!

Copyright

Dedication

To Remi.

You've never truly seen yourself as you are. Thank you for letting me hold up a mirror.

Your heart amazes me.

Acknowledgments

My writing process isn't simple. I've been incredibly lucky—and grateful—to have found a group of readers who don't mind my fits and starts. Who love to explore as I write instead of getting the story all at once. Who aren't afraid to nag me until they get the next installment. I cannot tell you how much they mean to me. I wouldn't want to write a book without them.

Thank you:

Ericka, Kelly, Kim R., Diana, Joeline, and Julia.

I owe you all the biggest hug if we are ever blessed to meet in person. Maybe two or three!

Chapter One

Remi —

Brown sugar and butter melted on my tongue, bringing a groan to my lips as I waited in the gloomy garage. Abby's oatmeal molasses cookies. The vague memories of my mother baking when Levi, Eli, and I were children didn't include the flavors of finished cookies, but if the memories were heaven, oatmeal molasses cookies would have to be in there somewhere.

I took another bite.

I'd popped the last bit into my mouth when I caught sight of her. Fulton County Memorial needed actual fucking lighting in here to keep their employees safe, but even in the dim light I knew it was Leah coming out of the elevator onto the third floor of the parking garage. My Leah. Everything inside me stood up and took notice, like a live wire buzzing through my veins. Lighting up every nook and cranny of my body. That's what she did to me every. Damn. Time.

Shifting to ease the suddenly tight stretch of denim across my dick, I picked up another cookie. Leah walked toward an old Toyota Camry with a booster seat in the back. A reliable car for a woman who didn't make much despite her long hours and compassion. Compassionate people rarely earned what they deserved; it was the bastards like me that got ahead in this world. I waited for her to pull toward the down ramp, just out of sight, then shoved the rest of the cookie in my mouth, cranked my nondescript SUV, and followed.

Atlanta traffic was a bitch any time of day, but trying to get out of town in the evening... She'd have no chance to lose me, even if she knew I was behind her. Gridlock had us inching our way south, and from the way she rode her brakes, I knew she was as impatient as I to escape. For far different reasons, but still. Her reason had blonde hair identical to hers, shades of yellow, caramel, and brown mingling together to provide a rich depth that made my fingers itch to touch it. Brown eyes just like hers too.

The child was six, I knew that. I knew her name and everything important about her, just like I did her mother. Not that either of them would ever know.

This far back, I couldn't catch a glimpse of those brown eyes in the rearview mirror. I wished I could. Every time I fucking saw her, I ached to stare into those eyes. They'd mesmerized me from the first moment I looked into them, drugged and disoriented from the coma, but Leah's dark eyes had stared down at me, grounded me, settled the fear in my gut.

There was nothing to settle the fear now, because that fear was reality—I'd never look into those eyes again. I would ache for her until I died, but I wouldn't give in. Leah and her child deserved a lot more in this life than a man with blood on his hands.

My cell rang as we exited the freeway at Union City. Leah's car headed west while I debated answering. I knew who was calling, and I knew he wouldn't be happy with me. He never was lately. Not that I gave a rat's ass, but I had no desire to waste time arguing.

I finally pressed the button on the console and answered. "Yeah?"

"Did the intel on our target pan out?"

No *hi, how are ya?* or even *how's it hanging, bro?* Levi was all business except on the rare occasions that his girlfriend, Abby, could trick him out of it. He'd raised me since I was ten, so I was used to it.

"It panned out," I told him. Butch Clarkson was definitely an abusive asshole. I didn't know who'd put a hit out on him, but he deserved everything he'd had coming his way. His wife was currently in a long-term care facility from a "fall down the stairs" that hadn't been an accident after all.

"Fine. Eli will start tracking his movements so we can—"

"Don't bother."

The silence that followed my words was heavy. Tense. Angry. And didn't faze me in the slightest.

"Why shouldn't I bother, Remi?"

"Because I took care of it." Clarkson would never throw another woman down the stairs. His associates wouldn't care, but I did.

Curses filtered through the speakers of the SUV. I barely paid attention, more interested in the little red Camry slowing ahead to turn into a neighborhood that was showing its age. The houses were a long commute from her work, smaller, with a bit more yard than new construction, but solid. Leah chose wisely, on a lot of things.

"I don't trust promises from men like you."

"Why the fuck would you do a job without full intel and without backup?" Levi growled, pulling me back from memories I should've buried a long time ago. "Are you trying to get yourself killed?"

The thought didn't bother me as much as it should have—a warning sign in my business. I brushed it off with a mental shrug. "I saw an opportunity and I took it. I knew all I needed to know."

"What I know is you have a fucking death wish. You're taking too many chances, Remi. You know better than that. *I taught you better than that.*"

You taught me a lot of things, big brother. Unfortunately lessons couldn't make you feel when all you wanted was to stop feeling.

I slowed, taking the same turn Leah had taken, far enough behind that she wouldn't notice. When she left the main road that bisected the neighborhood, I turned off my headlights and followed.

"This has got to stop, Remi."

Levi's words jerked me out of the fantasy of belonging in this little neighborhood with a woman and a little girl who deserved far better than me. He was right, too; he had no idea how right.

"You're risking too much and you know it. I can't lose you, brother. Either you rein it in or—"

"Or what?"

My words were deadly quiet. I could feel Levi's shock in the silence after them, knew he understood what I was saying—there was nothing he could do to stop me. I worked with my brothers because I wanted to, not because it was necessary.

The silence ticked by with the passing of car after car parked in front of each square of idealized domesticity. Levi finally spoke.

"Look, I love you; you know that. I even understand where you are coming from."

Because he knew about Leah. Or rather, about a woman; he didn't know her identity.

His voice went from gruff to dark and deadly, much as mine had been moments before. "But Remi, if you don't curb yourself, if you put Eli and Abby in danger, I will take care of business, don't you doubt it. I won't want to, but I will."

I didn't doubt it one bit. Levi would storm through hell to keep his woman safe. I knew because I felt the same. "Noted."

I clicked to end the call before either one of us could say something we really would regret—or before Levi could. I'd gone far beyond regret even before I took care of Mr. Wife Beater Clarkson.

Leah had parked in the driveway of a small gray house with weathered white trim. I pulled into a spot in front of a house catty-corner to hers, at just the right angle that I could see her fumbling to gather her things and get out of her car. I could see her walking up the sidewalk, her curves pulling my gaze down her body as she moved. I could see her sidestep to avoid the crack at the turn in the pavement just before the steps up to her porch. I didn't need to see any of it—I had watched her so many times that I knew each move by heart—yet I couldn't tear my gaze away.

And because I was watching, because I knew her body language better than my own, I saw the moment she hesitated outside the front entrance. Saw her keys fall from her hand to patter on the concrete before she yanked on the screen door.

Something wasn't right.

I was out of my car and crossing the street, heart pounding to the rhythm of my running feet, without a moment's hesitation. Leah's name escaped my lips over and over again, a mantra against the jacked-up fear I couldn't escape, no matter how irrational. It had been a single moment, one fleeting glimpse, but something inside me—instinct, paranoia, I didn't know what—said this wasn't irrational at all.

Put me in front of a gun with a round in the chamber and a finger on the trigger and my breath wouldn't even hitch. But Leah in danger? There was plenty of hitching. And swearing. And pleading with whatever spirit ruled the universe to keep her safe when I saw the broken-off knob on her screen door and the deep white gouges scarring the inner door's wood.

Someone had broken in—with Leah's child inside.

"Leah!"

Inside, chaos reigned though the room was empty. Furniture was out of place—the couch cushions split open, the coffee table overturned, the TV on its back as if its cabinet had been shoved. Toys and books and throw pillows were scattered among glass from a broken lamp and a teacup and plate shattered into pieces. Every drawer, every door was open as if someone had been searching for something.

I took it all in with one sweeping glance as I struggled toward the kitchen to the left. "Leah!"

The kitchen was empty as well, the destruction in the front room repeated here. A tornado had torn through the house, but still, I saw no sign of the people who lived here.

Until a startled scream came from one of the back rooms.

I cursed, stretching my long legs as far as they would go, taking the hallway like a sprinter with the finish line in sight. I hit the back bedroom in time to see Leah kneeling beside an older woman on the floor next to a heavy dresser. The angle of the woman's neck told me all I needed to know, but Leah couldn't read the story—one shaking hand was reaching to find a pulse.

I snatched her back before her fingers could make contact.

Chapter Two

Leah —

The hard hands grabbing me sent a jolt of terror through my already trembling body. Before I could spin around, an arm slammed across my ribs and I was jerked back against a strong, muscular chest. Strength like that couldn't be escaped—my father had taught me that. *Best way to defeat your attacker, Leah girl; just don't let him get his hands on you in the first place.*

Too bad I hadn't paid attention to my six. That didn't mean I wouldn't fight.

Nails. Heels. Fists. I threw everything I had—for nothing. This guy was like a brick wall, unmoving. The thought of the same hands on my daughter, of what they'd done to Lydia, only sent my panic higher. And then a hand clamped onto my mouth, too wide to bite, and the brush of stubble against the side of my neck threatened to undo me.

"Stop right now, Leah. You hear me? Be still and listen."

Oh God.

I squeezed my eyelids shut tight. It couldn't be. I'd imagined that voice too many times to count in the past year and a half, that same hot, heavy tone. It haunted me, that voice. Why would it be here now?

I'd gone still without meaning to—shock had a way of doing that. It allowed Remi to get a better grip on me, to drag me back from Lydia's body. And it was a body; I could see that now, see what my heart hadn't wanted to accept when I'd stepped into the room. None of the spirit that had made the woman a perfect partner in raising Brooke was present in the limp flesh lying on the floor. The angle of her head told the nurse in me that her neck was broken, likely from a fall against the secondhand dresser I'd found in a consignment shop—old, heavy.

My mind understood what it was seeing, but my heart… God, my heart hurt so much.

Where was Brooke? If something had happened to her in the fight, she'd be here, right? They wouldn't have taken her body…

The thought of my six-year-old as *a body* sent a sob into the hand over my mouth. Remi's arms gentled, molding me almost tenderly to that immovable chest despite the fact that he didn't let me go. That softness was nearly as dangerous as the force he'd used to begin with. Dangerous enough to break me.

I jerked my legs, the only part of me that was free, off the ground and kicked them back, bending my knees sharply. The toes of my shoes barely brushed his crotch before Remi spun me toward the blank wall beside the dresser. My face planted against the pale yellow paint, I struggled to breathe with the full weight of two hundred and fifty pounds of sheer muscle pressing me forward. A hard thigh slid between mine—

"For your protection and mine, Leah," he said.

But the rough, raw quality to his words and the surge of pleasure between my legs told another story.

I beat my forehead against the wall, and the pleasure faded. This wasn't the man I'd fantasized about in the bed across the room. This wasn't a romantic…whatever my libido was trying to imagine it was. Lydia was dead. Brooke was missing. It was sick to be thinking about anything else right now.

"I'm going to move my hand so you can talk, okay?" Remi said in my ear. He sounded strong, in control. Resentment sparked in my stomach, burning hot. I'd been under men's control before, and it never worked out well for me. But tonight I had to think about Brooke.

I nodded.

Remi removed his hand, his fingers sliding across lips, cheek, jaw, and coming to rest around my throat. Only slightly less threatening than before. I opened my mouth to point that out.

"Be careful," he warned me. "Be very careful, Leah."

So maybe not as in control as I'd thought. I had to swallow hard against the fear threatening to steal my voice. "Why?"

"Because I want to help you." He shifted behind me, and a heavy length pushing at the base of my spine flared into my awareness. "I can't to do that if you keep making trouble."

His words distracted me from his erection. "Why would you want to help me? Why are you even here?" I sucked in a deep, sudden breath, so sudden I choked. "You're a part of this, is that it? They left you here to confront me?" I jerked uselessly against his weight. "Where is my daughter?"

I felt more than saw his head shake. "I don't know where Brooke is. I'm not a part of this."

I attempted to throw a look over my shoulder, but the way he held me left no room to maneuver. "Why else would you be here?"

Remi took a deep breath, the expansion of his chest cutting off my air. On the exhale he eased back. "I'm not part of this. I can help you."

"You keep saying that." I peeled myself from the wall and turned just as carefully as he'd moved. "I'm not hearing another explanation."

Remi stood a few feet back, his arms locked over his chest, expression unreadable. This wasn't the man from my fantasies, the gruff but tender man I'd known for such a short time when he'd been injured. This man was hard. Cold. Dangerous.

I reached for my cell in my back pocket.

Remi watched, his gaze showing zero satisfaction when I found my pocket empty. He held up a hand— and my cell phone.

I reached for it. "I need to call the police, Remi."

He shook his head, keeping the phone just out of my reach. "She is beyond needing an ambulance and you know it," he said, jerking his chin toward Lydia. "The red tape cops would bring with them will only make it harder to find Brooke."

I forced my breath to stay even, my body still as my child's name left his lips. I hadn't spoken it aloud; I knew that. But Remi... "The only way you'd know her name was if you were involved. If you're not, give me the phone."

"I'm not involved."

"Then give me my phone. Now."

He slid the small black rectangle into his pocket. I lunged for it.

The next thing I knew, my hands were gripped in one of his and my jaw was in the other. He dragged me onto my tiptoes until I was almost level with him. "I'm not involved with whatever happened here," he bit out. "I promise."

I kneed him in the groin. Or tried to. Remi was prepared for everything, it seemed.

Fuck polite. Fuck complying with him—I went as crazy as I could with my hands in an unbreakable grip. Remi didn't take it lying down, but he didn't hurt me. Nor did he release my hands.

"Look," he barked, getting right in my face. "I don't know where Brooke is. I didn't take her. I don't know what the fuck is going on here—but I can't help you figure it out if you don't stop."

"It doesn't matter how many times you say it," I barked right back. "I don't believe you!"

Dragging me hard against him, he leaned in until his lips brushed mine and his golden-brown eyes were the only thing I could see. "I couldn't have done this because I wasn't here—I was following you home."

Following… "What?"

He released me, practically throwing my hands away. "I was following you from work. I came into the house after you. I couldn't have done this."

But my adrenaline-saturated brain wasn't getting it. "You followed me. From work?" I realized I was rubbing my aching wrists and forced myself to stop. *No sign of weakness.* "Why? How?" I shook my head hard. "How long have you been following me?"

"Long enough to know your daughter's name is Brooke. To know everything there is to know about her and you. What I don't know is who took her. At least not yet."

My stomach lurched, probably for a number of reasons—adrenaline, fear, confusion, and the sick certainty that my daughter was out there somewhere with someone who didn't care about her, someone who might hurt her. Someone who could disappear with her, and I would never see her again.

I barely made it to the hall bathroom before I threw up.

"Leah—"

"Out!" I shrieked. Surprisingly Remi retreated to the hall, giving me a few moments of semi-privacy to clean up the mess I'd made.

It wasn't until I began a quiet search of the cabinet for anything I could use as a weapon that he reappeared. "Not a good idea."

I allowed myself a moment to slump against the counter before straightening. "You're not going to convince me that you're a good guy, Remi. I've met your family, remember? They kidnapped me. You are fully capable of kidnapping a child. Just tell me where Brooke is and I'll do whatever you want."

A tick in his jaw was the only sign that what I'd just said might make him feel something, anything. Whatever it was, he fought it back. "I'm not going to waste time arguing with you anymore. You need to pack a bag."

"Why?"

"Because you can't stay here."

I threw up my hands. "And where do you suggest I go?" Not that I was going anywhere, especially with him. Brooke had been taken from here. I needed to be here in case her kidnappers came back. "I need to call the police, get them looking for her. I need to find her."

Remi grabbed the doorjamb on either side, the position both blocking my path and emphasizing the obscene size of his biceps and pecs. I forced my eyes to stay on his face, to stare him down no matter how much my insides felt like Jell-O.

"You already know what's happened to her, don't you?" he mused.

"I don't." And I didn't, not specifics anyway. That didn't mean I had no clue who was behind it. Hadn't feared something like this for years. I'd gotten complacent, though, allowed my guard down. Too soon, it seemed.

"You do," he said again, eyes narrowing when I tightened my lips. "You don't have to stay here, Leah. Whoever this is, they know how to get in touch with you. They will, when they're ready. Won't they?"

"And in the meantime?" I asked, ignoring his question. What was happening to my baby while they decided when they'd "be ready"?

"In the meantime—"

The ring of a phone cut Remi off, the sound originating from his pocket. Glancing from me to it, he fished the cell from his jeans and lifted it so I could see the white UNKNOWN flashing on the black screen. I reached for the phone.

"I don't think so," Remi said, pulling back just in time for my fingers to barely brush the edge. Turning the phone to himself, he clicked to answer the call, then clicked Speaker.

And waited.

"Leah?"

My heart slammed into my ribs. I staggered back to sit on the closed toilet seat, gripping the edges like they could keep me upright and sane—except I didn't think that was possible. Not anymore.

Chapter Three

Remi —

I narrowed my eyes on Leah's face, watching the color leach out, the way her hands came up, almost as if to ward something—or someone—off. She knew that voice. It scared her. Why?

"Who is this?" I used the tone that made marks shit their pants.

Silence. I could practically hear the man calculating, deciding on the best course of action. What I didn't hear was backing down.

"Oh, Leah," the man finally said. "You know better than to bring someone else into this."

"Where is Brooke?" she asked, voice trembling as much as her body. I could see it, see the fear gripping her. The need to pull her close, to comfort her, give her the safety of my arms, rose to choke me, but I forced it ruthlessly away. Now wasn't the time, nor would Leah welcome my touch.

"Brooke is safe," the man said. "Did you have any doubt?"

"You killed Lydia," she said, her tone all *hell yeah I doubt it.*

A heavy sigh crossed the line. He got her message loud and clear. He could read her just by her voice.

He knew her. Intimately. The thought blazed through my mind, hazing everything in red.

"An unfortunate accident," he was saying. "I didn't let Brooke see, I assure you of that. She is safe and sound."

"I want to speak to her," Leah said. "Please. Just let me tell her it's okay."

The little sob that said everything definitely wasn't okay tore at me, threatened to distract me even more than the jealousy. I'd never encountered that before—on a job I was all business; emotion wasn't a factor.

With Leah it was all emotion. Definite distraction.

"I always knew you'd be a wonderful mother," the man said. "But right now I don't think speaking to Brooke is the best idea. She's finally calm. Hearing Mommy's voice would undo all my hard work."

Hectic color hit Leah's cheeks. "You're a bastard."

"I'm not, Leah. You know I'm not."

A tear squeezed out as she closed her eyes, tearing at my gut, but there was no trace of weakness when she asked, "How did you find us?"

"An informant. He'd seen a news story a while ago, something about you being kidnapped?" Concern creeped in, making my skin crawl. "Everything turned out fine, it seems."

Leah scoffed. "Would you care if it hadn't?"

"How could you even ask me that?"

Leah tightened her lips in that way she had when she desperately wanted to say something but shouldn't. She knew him as well as he did her, then.

How well?

I shoved the question down deep. The caller was keeping this personal; getting down to business might throw him off. "What is it you want?" I asked.

Another pause—he didn't like talking to me. It proved my point. Finally he spoke, his tone almost tired. "Leah knows what I want; I'm sure she'll fill you in. She returns what belongs to a certain powerful someone, and she gets what belongs to her back safe and sound. That's it. Simple." Another sigh. "I'll be waiting, Leah."

The call clicked off.

As if her strings had been cut, Leah dropped to her knees on the floor, her body bowing down over her thighs. No matter how much my brain shouted that it was a bad idea, my heart forced me to go to her. Sobs threatened to choke her as she rocked forward and back, her face practically on the floor, crying her daughter's name—I couldn't stand it, couldn't leave her in so much fucking pain that it was ripping *my* guts out.

Kneeling down, I planted my knees on either side of hers and pulled her up into my arms, her face in the hollow of my shoulder, her tears soaking my shirt.

Holy shit.

I knelt there, her soft, trembling body against mine, and knew, in that moment, that I was lost. I had long ago decided never to walk back into her life. I could never be what she needed, except right now I actually was. Everything she needed.

I couldn't walk away from that.

And some damned part of me, down deep where I'd buried it alongside those memories of family and love and peace, was fucking ecstatic. I was holding the woman I loved in my arms for the very first time.

While she cried for her missing child.

Christ, I was a bastard.

The knowledge made my voice rougher than I wanted. "We need to go."

Leah shook her head against my chest.

I eased back, tilted her chin up until those liquid brown eyes met mine. "We need to go."

She blinked, still hazy. A pair of tears rolled down her cheeks.

I don't know what I was thinking; hell, maybe I wasn't thinking at all. I'd thought my instincts were all for killing, not for caring. But something I couldn't resist pushed me forward until my lips trapped a tear against her skin. My tongue snaked out to brush it away, to take the taste of her pain into my mouth. I moved to the other side and traced the path of her tears from jaw to eye, her lashes fluttering against my skin. When I straightened, so did she.

Our lips barely brushed each other.

Something powerful, something holy clenched my heart into a fucking knot behind my too-tight ribs.

"Leah"—I grabbed her arms and moved her away from me, telling myself I wasn't tearing a piece of me out while doing it—"we need to go." I made myself breathe, focus. "We can't find her tonight." At least not from here. Back home I had what I needed to get us started.

Leah looked anywhere but at me. Was she angry? Disgusted?

Did it matter?

"I can't—"

"You can." Pushing myself to my feet, I dragged her up with me. "What is it he wants? Is it here?" I doubted it considering the state of the house. Leah wouldn't keep something here that might draw danger to her daughter.

When she didn't answer, I gave her a little shake. "Is it?"

Making a visible effort to pull herself together, she wiped the backs of her hands across her eyes, smearing mascara as she went. She looked like she had been through hell and back—and she had—and still I had a hard time believing any woman could be so beautiful.

Would you get your mind on now and not your dick?

I dropped my hands. "Leah?"

Fists clenched at her side. She lifted her head to glare at me. "Go to hell, Remi."

I wanted to hear my full name on her lips—not the shortened version, but the whole thing, just once. I wanted her to say it when we were as close as we'd been moments ago. To say it when I was inside her. I wanted—

To hell with what I wanted. *Bastard, remember? Be the bastard you both need you to be.*

"I'm all you've got right now, so if I'm going to hell, you better pack for warm weather."

"I'm not leaving."

I raised an eyebrow. "You want to stay here with Mrs. Lydia?"

The words drained the fight from Leah's body—exactly what I'd hoped to accomplish. The stricken look on her face made me wish I could kick my own ass.

I forced my own anger out with a deep breath. "Look, I don't have anything here that can help you. I need you to come with me." I held up the phone. "They obviously know how to contact you."

She reached for the phone, and I slipped it back into my pocket. If she got ahold of it, I'd probably never see her again. At least if she had a say in it.

Which she didn't. Not right now.

She stared at the pocket where I'd tucked away her lifeline to her daughter. White teeth gleamed as she began to nibble at her bottom lip. I forced back a groan. Apparently it didn't matter what the situation was; anything Leah did made me tight and aching. All I could do was try to ignore it

"Do you have family you can contact?" I asked reluctantly. Brooke's father wasn't still in the picture, I knew that much—after over a year of watching, I'd never seen a sign of any man in Leah's life, thank fuck. I might've lost my shit long before now if I had.

Was he somehow involved with this?

I pushed the thought aside to examine later. "Do you have *anyone* you can contact who can help you like I can?"

Her dark eyes snapped to meet mine. "I can't get past the fact that I haven't seen you for a year and a half, Remi, and on the night my daughter is kidnapped, you miraculously reappear."

I shrugged. "Just because you haven't seen me doesn't mean I haven't seen you."

"Don't remind me. You're definitely not helping your case." She brought her hands up to rub her temples. "You have to be involved with this. There's no other logical explanation."

The words were weak, though, without the biting sting Leah could add when you pissed her off. She was holding on to the idea because it gave her some knowledge, some control in the midst of a confusing, chaotic world. I recognized the signs and couldn't blame her. She could hang on to whatever she needed to—as long as she came with me.

"Well"—I stepped aside, raised a hand to usher her toward the hallway—"if I'm involved, you'd better stick to me like glue. What better way to find your daughter?"

She stared me down a moment longer, brown eyes wary. And worried. When they dropped to the ground and she moved toward me, I knew I had won.

"All right," she said. "For now."

Chapter Four

Leah —

I didn't really care where Remi took me; all that mattered was being in close proximity to my phone. To the only lifeline I had to Brooke. Ross would call, and when he did, I needed to hear my daughter's voice. That's all I cared about now.

I had been staring, unseeing, out of the SUV's window for I don't know how long before we slowed and turned into a winding drive blocked by massive wrought-iron gates. Remi pulled to a stop and rolled down his window, waiting for the camera at the gate to recognize him. A buzz sounded, and the gate swung open. My gaze was on the massive stone house nearly a mile away, nestled in the arms of a forest on either side, as he drove through the entry.

"I agreed to come with you," I said, hoping he chalked up the anxiety in my voice to the past few hours. "I didn't agree to be put under lock and key with your whole family."

Because that had to be where we were. When your family now owned one of the most prestigious tech research firms, they could afford this kind of luxury. And security. I should feel safe behind those gates. Too bad someone far worse than Ross lived behind them too.

Remi let the car roll to a stop in the middle of the long driveway. "My family isn't who you need to fear, Leah."

"I beg to differ." Even if I was starting to believe Remi might not be involved in Brooke's abduction, I was a hundred percent certain his brother was fully capable of it. He'd kidnapped me before, after all.

To take care of his comatose brother. Remi had needed to be moved from the hospital after someone tried to finish the job they had started with the gunshot wound that almost killed him.

My head knew all that, but all I could remember were Levi's eyes. Those eyes had been dead, terrifying. They'd frozen me from the inside out. Being raised by a tough man had given me a certain amount of bravado, but I'd known the first time I saw Levi that he'd kill me and not blink an eye. He'd simply needed me at the time.

He didn't need me now. And Remi was taking me into the lion's den.

Remi reached across my lap, startling me. When the glove compartment popped open, he rummaged inside and pulled out a pen. Then he grabbed my hand.

"Remi, what—" I yanked my arm back, but the tug-of-war was short-lived. Turning my hand over, he wrote a series of numbers on the back.

"What are those?"

Remi clicked the pen off and tossed it back in the glove box, then slammed it closed. "That's the security code for the gate."

I eyed the black ink on my skin. Sure, it might get me out of the gate, but what about the house? Their surveillance? "I—"

Remi slammed both hands against the steering wheel. I jerked in my seat.

"I know you don't want my help, okay? You've made that loud and clear." Remi stared out the windshield, his profile fierce with anger and something else I didn't understand. "For once could you just let someone help you without arguing? Because I'm the best shot you've got at getting her back, Leah." He turned, his gaze searing into me. "I will absolutely get her back to you. I promise."

I don't trust promises from men like you. I had told him that once. The memory of those words lay between us in a kind of pregnant silence that Remi broke when he reached to cup my chin.

I flinched.

Remi frowned, his thumb gliding over my skin. I tried to ignore it, to tell myself I didn't feel anything. I tried to lie to myself—and couldn't.

"This is not like the last time," he finally said. "I know Levi used you, but not to hurt you; to keep me safe. I would've died without you." His gaze drifted to his thumb, stroking, stroking, stroking. "Let me repay that debt."

"You don't owe me anything, Remi." He hadn't been the one who kidnapped me.

"I owe you more than you know."

He dropped his hand and took his foot off the brake. The car rolled forward.

I didn't protest again.

He was wrong about one thing—I couldn't leave if I wanted to, not till my phone was back in my possession. And even then, where would I go?

My only consolation right now was knowing Ross was the one holding Brooke. I knew him, knew he wouldn't physically hurt her, just as he'd refused to hurt me seven years ago. Unlike some of Santo Fiori's other men. My baby was scared and alone but—for now, at least—she wouldn't come to harm. That didn't mean I would be anything but scared shitless until she was back in my arms again.

The massive front doors opened as Remi pulled the SUV to a stop in front of them. And there was Levi. I had to admit, he had the kind of dark good looks that helped you understand why the devil was the god of temptation. I had seen him with Abby Roslyn several times in the news since he'd stepped up to claim his family legacy, donating stunning amounts to local charities. A tux gave him just enough refinement that I could almost believe Abby had tamed him. Almost.

Except the eyes didn't lie. And if there was one thing I knew with absolute certainty, it was that suits and uniforms didn't make you a good guy.

Levi seemed intent on proving my point as he barged down the shallow steps to the driveway. He drew up short when I opened my door and stepped out.

Nice to know something can take you by surprise, big guy.

"What the fuck is she doing here?"

Remi rounded the SUV with lazy grace, but I knew better than to trust the seemingly casual approach. The tension in the air reminded me of two bulls facing off, ready to gore each other to the death.

The sight actually calmed me like nothing else could. Sure, they might be acting for my benefit, but I didn't think so. Levi hadn't known I was coming. Remi hadn't told him, and looked ready to fight to get me inside.

Don't believe it, girl. Just don't. I'd learned my lesson about bad boys with Angelo. And yet I couldn't deny the warmth creeping into my body in places that should stay ice-cold around Remi.

Yes, I really was a total idiot.

"She's here because I brought her here," Remi said.

Levi's curses had me going tense again.

"Why, for fuck's sake?" He glared at me. "This is our home, Remi. Our safe place. Why would you bring an outsider here?"

Remi's lips tightened as if holding back words. I shifted a leg back, bracing myself, though I wasn't sure what for.

"Her daughter was kidnapped," Remi finally said.

Levi cursed again—that seemed to be his primary mode of communication today, though I knew he was capable of far more—and scrubbed a hand over his face. "That doesn't mean you have to bring her here."

"Leah, grab your bags."

"Remi—"

Remi charged toward his brother, and I hurried to bury my head in the SUV. He'd insisted I pack some things, so I had a small suitcase, a backpack with things for Brooke—which I *would* need, very soon, I promised myself—and my purse. By the time I had gathered it all and shut the back hatch, Levi was throwing his hands up and turning for the doors. Remi ignored him and came to take the suitcase and backpack out of my hands.

"Thank you." For taking on my burdens or defending me to Levi, I wasn't sure, but I had precious little to be thankful for right now, so I'd take either one.

Remi grunted a reply before ushering me inside.

The double doors opened onto a wide-open foyer that blended into living areas on both sides. Lined with floor-to-ceiling windows, the whole place was flooded with light. I caught my breath at the beauty of it. Only money could capture elegance and warmth the way this house captured it. I had been raised on a cop's salary by a single dad; money had been scarce, as had beauty like this.

Remi whisked me through the open space to a staircase, past the second floor to a third. We turned right toward a long hallway with several doors opposite darkly tinted windows. Remi led me to the first one.

Inside was a room in soft cream with blue bedding and drapes. "This is my wing," Remi said. "Eli has the opposite side, and the second floor is Abby and Levi's."

"I'll avoid that floor."

Remi ran a hand through his thick hair, his raised arm once again drawing my eyes to thickly cut biceps. "Levi's protective of his family."

"I got that when he ordered Eli to kidnap me from the hospital after I helped get you out."

"I'm sorry."

And he was—I could read the regret in his eyes. "Don't be. You didn't take me away from my daughter; you were unconscious."

"And now someone has taken your daughter from you."

I shrugged, desperate to hide the surge of fear that rose whenever Brooke entered my mind. If I was paranoid, I might wonder why these things kept happening to me. There was no reason to wonder, though. I knew exactly why Ross had come for me. The answer to that question had come far before Brooke was born. What I didn't know was what to do about it.

I glanced around the sparse but elegant room. "I know who you are, you know," I said softly, carefully. "I saw the story a few months ago about your parents on the news." My hands fisted in my pockets. "I never said anything."

"I know."

Of course they did. If I'd said something to the authorities, they would've been notified. Money guaranteed certain privileges.

"So now you live here. Doing…what?"

What was I trying to ask him? If his brother still killed people for a living? Were they all retired? I shouldn't want to know, but I did.

"Yes, we live here now." Remi grinned, the curve of his lips causing my heart to skip a beat. "Just your average, everyday millionaire family." He shrugged. "You know how that goes."

I definitely didn't. "Millionaires with plenty of skeletons in your closets," I couldn't resist adding.

Probably literal skeletons. Remi's family company had been the site of a shooting a few months ago, the former CEO of Hacr Tech the victim. Police blamed the incident on an embezzlement scheme gone wrong and arrested the family lawyer. If the man had embezzled from the family, I had a feeling the lawyer would be the last person delivering justice.

Remi set my bags on the bed. "Or in the basement."

I refused to ask if the house had a basement. I really didn't want to know any more than I already did. Or at least that's what I told myself.

So why did I keep asking questions?

"Get a shower, change," Remi told me. Without another glance, he headed for the door. "I have a few things I need to check. Then we've got to talk, Leah, and I mean really talk." Hand on the doorknob, he turned to look at me. "You need to tell me everything you know about this man and what he wants. No secrets. I can't help you if you keep secrets from me."

He left the room, the door clicking shut behind him. I stared at it for a long time, wondering what to tell him. How to tell him. I'd prayed this day would never come, when my past returned to haunt me, but there was no getting around it.

Getting Brooke back meant revealing everything. I had nowhere else to turn, no one else who could help me. I just prayed Remi didn't use what he learned against me.

Chapter Five

Remi —

Seeing her here, in the house I'd grown up in, the house we'd made our home in the last few months, was a kick to the gut. I wouldn't pretend I hadn't fantasized about it, usually in the aftermath of a far more visceral fantasy, but no way in hell had I ever believed it would happen. I'd never have wished for a little girl to be stolen away from her mother, but I wouldn't be sorry that Leah was here with me.

Even if it meant facing off with my big brother. Levi had only backed off because I had promised to explain everything as soon as I got Leah settled. Which meant I was headed down to the bat cave right now.

Yes, we called our basement office the bat cave.

We had lived out of so many safe houses through the years, never putting down roots, always ready to abandon everything at a moment's notice. It still felt surreal to realize it would literally take an army to breach this place, that we could actually *relax* here. I wasn't sure I'd ever get used to it. I found myself leaving as often as I could, unable to get rid of the itch between my shoulder blades. My brothers, though, seemed to have settled right in.

Which was why Levi was so pissed about having a guest.

The elevator whisked me down to the basement level with no more than a whisper of movement. Stainless steel doors opened on a room with soft blue walls and enough recessed lighting that a cave was the last thing I thought of when I saw it. It wasn't the room itself that gave us the name—it was what was in it.

Every possible piece of high-tech equipment known to man. Screens scattered along the walls with active maps, data streaming, and surveillance. A massive walk-in safe built into one wall, serving as a weapons locker that was every mercenary's wet dream.

And an electronics corner with all the latest gaming equipment. A man had to have a few vices. Or Eli did, anyway.

I strode over to the couch where my younger brother sat, controller in hand, eyes glued to the flaming race car on the screen. A smack upside the head got his attention.

"Hey!"

"Need you, bro," I said.

"We got another job?" He paused the game and tossed his controller onto the low coffee table. "I'd be surprised if Levi lets you off the chain again for a very long time after jumping the gun on Mr. Clarkson."

"News spreads fast." Although maybe not fast enough, since Eli hadn't mentioned Leah. "Not another job. Come with me."

The sound of the elevator doors opening preceded Levi's furious stride across the concrete floor. Abby had insisted on rugs in several places "to keep the place from becoming as frigid as a meat locker," to which Levi had replied that his meat was never cold—and Eli and I had gagged him—but the rest of the room was still polished concrete. Sometimes you just needed noisy boots on solid rock to get your aggression out.

Levi more than most of us.

I braced myself.

"All this time, it was the fucking nurse? That's who you were jerkin' off for?"

The words were no sooner out of his mouth than I had a forearm across his throat and his body slammed against the cinder block wall. Levi was big, we all were, but I carried twenty pounds more muscle than either of my brothers and I wasn't afraid to throw it around when necessary.

Levi choked, his eyes flashing with anger, but he didn't fight back. I almost wished he would.

I leaned in close. "Never disrespect her again. Got me?" He would never allow us to say something like that about Abby. Leah might not be here for long, but she'd been mine since the moment I first opened my eyes and met hers. No one would insult her in front of me.

Levi raised his hands out to his sides. "I got you," he croaked.

I leaned in harder for good measure before letting him go.

"What nurse?" Eli asked.

"Leah Marrone," I said.

Eli's eyes became saucers. "You didn't."

"I did." Why did everyone find it so hard to believe that the woman I was interested in was Leah?

Maybe because she's far too normal for you. Or because she's seen your family's bad side, and no way would she willingly come back.

I knew that better than anyone.

Levi cleared his throat. "Fill us in, Remi."

"Her daughter was kidnapped."

"What the hell?" Eli shoved a hand through the thick blond hair that was a twin to mine. "How?"

Levi shook his head. "We'll get to that." His gray gaze bored into me, drilling deep with ice-cold precision. That look had kept me in line when we were only young punks living on the streets; now he used it to make me spill my guts. "Tell me about her."

I stared at my brothers. I trusted them with my life, always had. But Leah... She'd been my secret for so long. Not because I was ashamed or guilty, but because she'd been a dream, something I knew I'd never really have. Why bother talking about it?

Now... I wanted to. I needed to.

I walked to the conference table and took a seat. My brothers followed.

"I—" Shit. Now that the time had come, I had no clue how to explain the unexplainable. "I couldn't forget her," I finally said. Completely inadequate, but...

"Then why haven't we seen her since?" Eli asked. We—or rather, Eli and Levi—had released her as soon as I awoke from the coma and stabilized.

I snorted. "Right. I'll just walk up to her and ask for a date. 'Really, my brothers are okay guys. I know they kidnapped you, but give me a chance.'"

Eli grinned at my falsetto explanation. "Why not?"

But it was Levi who studied me, seeing far more than I was ready to reveal. "You've been following her."

I dropped my gaze to the tabletop. Men like us, assassins, weren't supposed to have weaknesses. And a woman you can't stop thinking about, can't control the urge to be near, was a hell of a weakness.

"Yes."

Levi didn't curse; I'd almost rather he did. Silence said he was thinking far too hard.

"What happened to her daughter?" Eli asked, seeming oblivious to our older brother's stony look.

While I explained what I knew, I could see Levi working it out in his brain, see Eli's fingers twitch with the need to start digging. In a sense this was what we did. Yes, that usually involved killing people, but it was more about justice than murder or money. That was how Levi had raised us, how he had maintained his integrity when he'd had no one to rely on but himself.

Never harm the innocent. The guilty are fair game.

"We need to get a cleaner to Leah's, move the nanny's body to her home," I said finally.

"We'll worry about that later," Levi said, voice gravelly. "Where is your surveillance?"

Of course he'd know; he always knew. "Upstairs."

He jerked a nod. "Reroute it down here, ASAP. Have you got outside only or—"

"Outside only." I had refused to let myself go so far as to invade the privacy of Leah's home. Probably a ridiculous line to draw since I had essentially been stalking her, but... I gave a mental shrug as I moved to a bank of computers and got to work.

A few minutes later the footage taken at the time of the kidnapping was up and ready to go.

Levi planted a fist on the desk next to Eli, with me on the other side. "Roll it."

I clicked the Play button, and we all watched as a darkly tinted SUV pulled into Leah's driveway. Two men got out, one tall with blond hair, dressed in khakis and a button-down. Very casual except for the bulge under his sports coat that said he was packing. The second man, dark hair, wore a black suit and too-fancy dress shoes to go with his multiple guns. Neither man made an effort to hide their faces as they walked toward the porch.

"Pause," Eli said when they stepped in front of the door. They were directly facing a camera too small for them to detect with the naked eye.

I moved aside and let Eli work his magic. Our youngest brother was the most tech savvy. He had screen captures of the men's faces and was running facial recognition faster than I could nail an unmoving target.

I hit Play again.

The men didn't pause for more than a minute at the door. They didn't knock either. Fancy Man pulled out a metal rod, leveraged it against the glass door's handle, and yanked. The same rod gouged into the wood of the front door to pry it away from the jamb.

The scene went blank as they moved inside.

"The nanny is dead, from a fall against the dresser in the back bedroom. Probably trying to get Brooke out a back window."

"And Leah hasn't told you what it is the men were looking for?" Levi asked.

"Not yet." She would, though.

The computer beeped, a small box popping up on screen. Eli elbowed me out of the way.

"The guy with the fancy pants has an arrest record in DC." He typed furiously, the screen changing too fast for me to track as multiple programs ran. "Seems there are rumors he has ties to the Fiori family up there."

"The mob?" Levi asked.

"Yep."

I swore under my breath. What the fuck could the mob want with a woman like Leah?

You don't really know what kind of woman she is, do you?

Yes, I had followed her, searched for public records, that kind of thing, but I hadn't gone too deep. Deep meant finding out about her life with another man. I might be a glutton for punishment, but I wasn't sure I could handle picturing her happy with someone, lying beneath someone, delivering her child while another man held her hand.

Levi's gaze burned into me. I caught myself before I could squirm in my seat like an untried teen.

"What the hell is she into?" he asked.

I forced myself to meet his eyes. I'd brought Leah into our lives—this time—and I was responsible for whatever came with her.

"I don't know, but I'll find out."

Levi's look promised he would if I didn't. I couldn't blame him. A small nod was all I could manage.

A sharp whistle drew our attention back to Eli.

"Blondie has an interesting story."

"Yeah?" I leaned in. "Tell me."

"He's a cop."

"A cop and a mob enforcer working together?" Levi asked.

"To kidnap a child?" I added.

"And not just any cop." Eli brought up a news story from a local DC newspaper. The headline, SERVICE RUNS IN THE FAMILY, was dated ten years ago. The cop, Ross Windon, had received a commendation for his work on a national drug task force.

And pictured right at the top was Windon and an older man, also in uniform, surrounded by officials.

Shit.

Levi reached past me to point at the background where a young teen stood, clapping and smiling. A teen with rich blonde hair and a smile that hadn't changed much in a decade.

Pictured left to right: Ross Windon, Police Commissioner Ross Windon Sr., and Leah Windon at awards ceremony.

The caption hit me like a gun butt to the head. "That's not her name."

It was stupid, I know. Names changed. Maybe Leah and Brooke's father had married. Except there was no public record of either a marriage or a name change.

"Unfortunately," Eli said, clicking through more screens, "it was. I don't know how or why, but it was."

"How are they related?" Levi asked. The dark undertone of his voice made my skin crawl because the threat was directed toward the woman I loved. Or thought I loved. Except I didn't really know her, and she was a threat to our family. A threat I'd invited in.

"He's her brother."

We're not supposed to show weakness, but I closed my eyes for the briefest moment. She'd cried after the call, but not since. She'd been oddly calm, actually.

Because she knew her brother had Brooke? Because she thought her daughter was physically safe?

And she hadn't told me, had in fact led me to believe her daughter's kidnapper might not be able to find her if she left the house.

She'd lied. And I was about to find out why.

Chapter Six

Leah —

I'd worked a twelve-hour shift, struggled through the destruction of the home I'd built for my daughter and me, Brooke's kidnapping, the death of one of the only friends I had allowed myself to have. When the door closed behind Remi, leaving me alone in the silent room, all of that came flooding back. Suddenly I couldn't stand the clothes touching my body, the sweat and dirt and memories. I'd taken a shower at the hospital after my shift, but after everything that had happened, I couldn't get my clothes off fast enough.

After grabbing a fresh set from my suitcase, I hurried into the adjoining bathroom. The colors from the bedroom had been carried over, calming cream walls and deep blue tile. I set my clothes on the counter, stripped, and took advantage of the new toothbrush and toothpaste waiting on the counter before turning the water in the shower on to heat.

The tears hit when I stepped beneath the spray.

I tried to hold them back. Crying was a weakness I couldn't afford. Hell, I had gone through my entire pregnancy, labor, and delivery with no one to hold my hand, share the burden, prop me up when I felt like I couldn't take another step. I was strong. Crying didn't make you strong, and it sure as hell didn't help you fight.

But I couldn't make them stop. Twice in one day, damn it.

I should be sitting beside Brooke on her bed, the two of us making slow progress on her latest chapter book, her warm body getting heavier as she drifted into sleep against my side. I should be tucking her in beneath the soft pink and yellow comforter she'd chosen when she turned five and moved from a toddler bed to her very own "big girl" twin-size. I should be watching her eyelids flutter, those long, long lashes she'd inherited from her father brushing her cheeks as she slept.

Would Ross tuck her in? Was she crying herself to sleep without her mommy to hold her in a strange place. He might not be hurting her, but what about her fear, her panic, her hunger, her need. What would he do to stop those?

Jesus, I wanted Brooke in my empty arms right now.

I leaned my forehead against the chilled tile and let go. *Just let it all out.* Clear the decks, my dad used to say. Get it over with, then get back to finding her.

The logical part of my brain was right. I cried until I gagged, cried until my tear ducts ran dry and the endorphins had run their course, and then I washed myself from head to toe, rinsing off the fear and grief. By the time I turned the never-ending stream of hot water off, I was ready for battle.

With Remi or Ross, I wasn't sure. Whichever I had to, I guess.

My dirty clothes went into the trash can—*never wearing those again*—and my clean clothes went on my body one piece at a time. The only armor I had. I walked from the bathroom into the bedroom determined to find Remi and figure out what we could do to find Brooke right this minute—

Only to draw up short.

"Hello."

Abby Roslyn was arranging a tray on the table in the corner. The scent of warm bread and cookies registered in my nose about the time my gaze settled on the thick sandwich, chips, and dessert she'd brought in. A rumble hit my stomach seconds later.

Abby smiled. "I thought you might need something to eat." The smile collapsed into a frown as her gaze brushed my face, no doubt noting the redness and distress I couldn't hide. "I understand it's been a stressful evening. I'm sorry."

Abby had never had children as far as I knew—and yes, I looked her up after Levi and Eli had released me. She had been my fellow captive, after all, though she'd seemed content to stay with the men by the time I'd met her. She couldn't relate to missing her child, but she knew what it was like to be kidnapped, so I took the sympathy as genuine.

"I am sorry too." So damn sorry my life had come back to haunt us, to harm Brooke. Moving toward the table, I settled a hand on my growling stomach. "The food is definitely appreciated. Thank you."

Abby took the seat opposite me as I settled in to eat. "Levi said they'd be up shortly to talk. I thought I'd get you fueled up first."

"For the interrogation?"

It was only partially a joke. With Remi, I'd believe we were just going to talk. With Levi? *Interrogation* might be putting it mildly.

"We want to help you, Leah."

I sighed. She probably did. Unfortunately I didn't trust the man she was involved with one inch.

"You live here now?" I asked, hoping to take her focus off me.

"I do," she said.

Something of the Atlanta socialite came through in her answer. Though she didn't spend as much time in the spotlight as she had when her father was alive, she'd been raised to wealth and privilege. This mansion eclipsed the home Derrick Roslyn, then a gubernatorial candidate, had died in, but it probably felt far more normal to her than it did to me.

I took a bite of the sandwich and chewed. How normal did her relationship with Levi feel?

"And yes," Abby said, seeming to read my mind, "Levi and I are together."

"You didn't take my advice then." Not that I'd expected her to. She was young. Levi was a bad-boy alpha male with occasional glimpses of normalcy. Of course she was susceptible.

Abby planted her elbows on the table, surprising me. Chin cradled in her hands, she said, "I know him, Leah."

I'm sure you think you do. I popped a chip in my mouth.

I understood the appeal; after all, I had been caught in the same web with Angelo. We might even have ended up in a similar place. But Angelo had ended up dead, and I'd had my entire life stripped away. There were no illusions left for me to indulge.

Abby leaned back in her chair. "I never got to thank you for helping Remi."

"I didn't have much of a choice." Not that I regretted helping him, not really.

And what the hell was wrong with me? Antagonizing the woman wasn't going to get me anywhere. I needed every ounce of help I could get.

I needed to shut my mouth.

I did, with another bite of sandwich.

Abby shook her head. "You still hold a grudge; I get it. But you didn't report anything either, so don't try to pretend you didn't understand why he did it."

I threw down my napkin. So much for diplomacy. "Of course I understand why he did it. What I don't understand is your willing blindness toward a man who is a straight-up killer. You think he loves you—"

"He does."

"I thought the same, a long time ago." Angelo wouldn't have given his life for a woman he didn't love. "And maybe he truly does, Abby. That doesn't mean that at some point his lifestyle won't get you killed."

A vee creased Abby's forehead. "Is that what happened with your daughter's father?"

Your daughter. Brooke wasn't just my daughter; she was a human being, and they needed to see her that way. See her as valuable.

"Brooke," I said, fear thickening the word. "Her name is Brooke."

Something soft sparked in Abby's gaze. She nodded. "Brooke's father?"

I stared at her a moment. I'd never told anyone the whole story with Angelo, not even Ross. My father didn't know he had a granddaughter, or if his own daughter was still alive. He'd never have understood the whole story, but Abby…

Standing up, I left the table behind to pace the length of the room. "I met Angelo when I was seventeen."

Abby turned in her seat to face me. "You were young."

A grin tugged at my lips. "And naive. He came into the coffee shop where I worked." The memory of the first time I'd seen him standing in line, his sharp gaze pinning me in place, still sent a shiver through my body. Based on my reaction to him, and to Remi, and the lack of response to any other man in between, I definitely had a type.

Too bad for me.

"He was older, in his thirties, but the moment I saw him, I knew…" I shook my head. "It was love at first sight." I still couldn't believe he was gone. It seemed unreal even now.

"So you started dating?"

I shook off the horror creeping in at the corners of my mind. "We did. I didn't tell my family—my dad was protective, probably because we lost my mom when I was a little girl. And I didn't want anything to ruin this shiny new happiness that had taken over my life.

"It wasn't until I found out I was pregnant that he told me he worked for the mob."

Abby's gasp made me chuckle.

"I told you," I said, "I understand the appeal."

"What happened?"

I met her eyes, and I knew she could guess the end of my story.

"He died."

"Jesus, Leah. I'm so sorry."

I turned toward the darkened window. Night had fallen hard, but the lawn outside was lit with a myriad of lights. Security, of course. You can't stop a threat you didn't see coming. "It was a long time ago."

And now it was coming back to harm the family Angelo had given his life to protect.

"I think Angelo and Levi are a lot more alike than you want to acknowledge," Abby said. "They both love, or loved"—she winced—"their women. Their families. Levi would do anything to protect me, just as Angelo was willing to do for you."

I couldn't hold back a laugh at that, though the sound wasn't the least bit amused. "Oh, I have no doubt about that. The problem is, they can't protect you from everything."

"Leah—"

I threw up a hand. "Just stop, Abby, okay? You're not going to convince me that Levi's the good guy here. I don't even believe Remi is a good guy. I don't trust any of you."

A stricken look crossed the redhead's face, but I hardened my heart, forced myself to ignore it.

"If you don't want to be here, if you don't want our help, why don't you leave? What about your family?"

I barely held back a snort. "I don't have any." Not that I would draw into this, anyway.

The door opened behind me. I turned, the sight of Remi taking my breath in that way I hated but couldn't seem to avoid. And then his expression registered.

Uh-oh.

"Don't have any what?" he asked, voice deceptively calm.

"Family," Abby answered for me. Probably a good thing since my tongue was stuck to the roof of my mouth.

"Hmm..." Remi's eyes narrowed on me, the pure rage shining there drawing me like the beauty of a King Cobra about to strike. "That's not entirely true, is it?"

Chapter Seven

Remi —

Leah had lied to me. The thought reverberated in my brain even as I watched shock flare in her eyes. It wasn't so much that she hadn't told me the man on the phone was her brother; it was everything else. I'd been so blinded by my feelings for her that I hadn't thoroughly vetted the person I had brought into my family's home.

I'd put my family at risk—for a woman.

The knowledge filled me with rage.

"Tell me, Leah."

Abby was silent, seated at a table in the corner, her lips tight as she watched us. I heard my brothers enter the room behind me. They always had my back, even when I majorly fucked up. God, how I'd fucked up.

I stalked Leah across the room, my anger and the bulk of my body pushing her back until her spine hit the wall. "Tell me."

The impact jolted her out of her shock. "Tell you what?" she asked.

"Tell me about your family." My words came out gravel-rough, sharp edges cutting. "You do have one, I know you do, so don't bother lying anymore."

Her eyes went wide. "What are you talking about?"

For a moment I wished I didn't have to do this, wished Leah and I could somehow disappear to a place where the world couldn't touch us and we could just be normal, have a chance at something beyond secrets and the danger they brought with them. But normal had passed me by as a child, and I was beginning to suspect Leah hadn't been far behind. I held up the printout. "Care to tell me about him?"

Her gaze dropped to the paper. Had I not known his background, I still would've known the man was related to her—it was in the shape of their eyes, the fullness of their mouths that was too feminine on Ross and just right on Leah. The chin that was slightly squared off, heavier on Ross than his sister. Even their coloring favored each other.

There was no doubt they were related; I simply needed Leah to admit it to me herself. But she stood, frozen, eyes transfixed by the sight of the man in the picture, her mouth open as if to speak.

Nothing came out.

Something snapped. My hands fisted, my knuckles slamming into the wall on either side of Leah's head. A strong arm snaked around my throat, yanking me back—one of my brothers; I didn't care which, only that their grip jolted me out of my rage. Out of the need to get in my woman's face and roar until she told me why she'd lied to me. I needed to force the truth out of her, one way or another—

And that lack of control was completely unacceptable.

The grip on my neck tightened, an anchor grounding me when I felt lost in the sea of emotion. I focused on it, on now, on reality. Leah was a threat, and I knew how to deal with threats.

Assassin's Heart

A double tap to the arm had it easing off. Eli, I realized. Giving him a nod of thanks, I turned back to Leah. "Sit down," I barked.

Hands gripping her elbows, face white, Leah complied. She didn't look at Abby or my brothers, her dark eyes riveted solely on my face, waiting for my next command. I'd let her wait.

When the silence had stretched to the breaking point, I spoke. "You are going to tell us everything you know, Leah. Everything. Start with your real name."

Abby's gasp echoed the shock I'd felt earlier. I wasn't shocked anymore; I was pissed.

Leah's hard swallow was audible. "Leah is my real name."

"You don't want to play games right now," Levi said next to me, his words arctic. "Tell us what we want to know."

Leah's wide eyes shifted to him for a long moment before she slumped back in her seat. "My name is Leah Windon."

"Why isn't there any record of a name change?" I asked.

"You already know why," she said wearily.

I did. I knew she was on the run. The question was, from what.

"This man"—Eli waved a hand at the paper I still held—"is your brother, Ross Windon Junior."

A statement. We knew he was; she couldn't deny it.

She didn't try this time. Instead she stared at the face, shadows drifting in her gaze. "He is."

The short answer gave away nothing. She was going to lead us around like dogs, barely giving anything away, wasting time we didn't have. I was done.

"Enough!" I yelled, satisfaction seeping in when Leah's eyes became saucers. "Stop fucking around and tell us the whole story, or I'll escort you to the gate and you can find Brooke on your own."

It was an empty threat; even with my head filled with a red haze and a fucking two-ton anvil sitting on my chest, I knew that much. My mother had been taken from me when I was ten. I could never leave a child separated from her mother if I had the power to fix it.

That didn't mean threats weren't effective every once in a while, no matter how empty. As Leah proved.

Her entire body rounded in on itself, her gaze dropping to the hardwood floor. "Yes, he's my brother." She paused, cleared her throat. "We were raised in DC."

"By the police commissioner," Levi pointed out.

"He wasn't the police commissioner when we were kids. That came later."

"But Ross is a cop as well."

"He is." Leah shook her head. "My dad has nothing to do with this, I promise. If he knew..." She raised beseeching eyes to me, eyes that touched me despite my efforts to block them out. "This would kill him."

I fisted the paper in my hand, satisfaction filling me as it crumpled beneath the pressure. "Start from the beginning and tell us everything."

Leah stood. I tensed, but she only began to pace the length of the room. Trying to get her thoughts together? I forced myself to watch her expression, searching for any hint of a lie, rather than watching the easy grace of her body as she moved. How could I notice something like that and be as angry as I was? It made no sense, but then my feelings for this woman had never made sense.

"Angelo, Brooke's father, and I met when I was seventeen." She glanced at Abby, and from the look on Abby's face, they'd discussed this already. "He was much older. We fell in love immediately."

The knife in my heart was harder to ignore than her body.

She shrugged, a self-deprecating smile curving her lips. "I had no idea what he did for a living; I didn't care. There were so much more important things to think about."

Like sex. I didn't want to go there. Unfortunately my brain seemed intent on torturing me.

"We'd been together for a few months when he told me he was an enforcer for the Fiori family. By then I was pregnant." Leah's chuckle came out strained. "The police commissioner's daughter, raised to excellence, to service, to justice, pregnant by a mob enforcer."

"Your family didn't suspect?" Abby asked quietly.

"No. God, no."

"But your brother is in on this," I pointed out. There were a lot of ways a cop could be turned, but a commissioner's son…

"That came later." Leah turned to the window, and I noticed her palm smoothing over her belly. "We hadn't meant to get pregnant, but Angelo… He wanted the baby so much, wanted us to get married, be a family, but I refused to put my child in danger."

Up and down, over and over, her hand stroked her belly, right where her baby had been. "He could get out, he said."

Levi and I exchanged a look. With the mob there was no getting out, except in a pine box.

"He kept telling me I just needed to be patient," Leah was saying. "So I tried to be. I wanted to believe him." Her eyes sparkled, unshed tears catching the artificial light as it filtered through the window.

"What did he do?" I asked, the sight of her pain and my own lingering anger roughening the words.

She turned to lean a shoulder against the wall. "He'd made recordings, apparently."

Curses rang through the air. My brothers knew as well as I did that this wouldn't end well.

Leah ignored our response. "He told his boss he was leaving, that the recordings would never see the light of day if they just left him alone. And that's what they seemed to do." She shrugged. "I realized later they were just biding their time, watching, waiting. They wanted the tapes, and they'd use anything they could to get them.

"One night they broke into Angelo's apartment." A shudder rocked her body. I wanted to go to her, make the memory stop, soothe the turmoil ravaging her—but I couldn't. That intimacy wasn't mine to take. That closeness would only lead to more mistakes. I wouldn't risk my family again.

"They…" Leah brought her fingers to her mouth, covering their trembling as she visibly pulled herself together. "They tortured him. In front of me. And when that didn't work, they started on me." Leah's eyes went blank, her focus somewhere in the past. "Angelo managed to break free. He fought them so that I could get away. And they killed him."

"But they knew you were involved," Eli said where he sat on the end of the bed. "They would come after you."

"They did. So I went to the only person I thought I could trust to help me."

The weight on my chest shifted from anger to dread. "Your brother."

Leah looked down, her hair sliding forward to conceal her expression. To hide her innermost thoughts from me. "My brother."

"He was recognized for his work on a national drug task force," Levi pointed out. "That's how the mob found him?"

"Yes." Leah raised her head, squared her shoulders. "They found him and they flipped him."

He'd been working both sides. What better way to control what the local police knew, to learn of possible actions against them, than to own the commissioner's son?

"He kept telling me if I would just hand over the recordings, everything would be fine. That's what he said, fine." A laugh escaped her. "What he meant was, he would protect me if I would just cooperate." Her eyes met mine for the first time since I'd walked into the room, allowing me to see the burn of determination flaring there. "I saw what they did to Angelo. I refused to trust my child's future to a traitor. So I ran."

Successfully, too. She'd hid herself well enough that a well-connected cop and a dangerous mob hadn't found her. On top of that, she'd had all the struggles of a more typical single mom—caring for a child, educating herself, finding work and supporting them both.

Christ, Leah. Who held your hand when you delivered Brooke? Was there ever anyone there for you?

"Ross said an informant told him about you being on the news," I reminded her, as much for my brothers' benefit as anything else. "We are the ones who exposed you." It was important that everyone knew that, our role in this problem.

And she had every reason to blame us, but that wasn't what I saw in her eyes when they met mine.

"It is what it is, Remi. I just want my daughter back."

"So we hand over the recordings and you get Brooke back safe and sound," Levi said.

"Do you really think it's going to be that easy?" The look in Leah's eyes said she didn't.

Levi's brow scrunched together. "I think your brother came here instead of sending mafia thugs to kill his sister and niece and take what they want. Ross obviously doesn't want the two of you hurt; some protective instinct still lives in there. Just give him the recordings."

"I can't."

The four of us glanced at each other before staring back at Leah. "Why not?" I asked.

The arms around Leah's middle clenched, holding her together. "Because I don't know where Angelo kept them. I never have. And they'd never believe that. That's why I had to run."

Chapter Eight

Leah —

It was past midnight before I insisted everyone leave. We weren't going to figure out in a few hours what I hadn't figured out in seven years, and I'd spent plenty of time thinking about it. Sometimes I wondered if the recordings had even existed.

I hoped to God they did; otherwise Fiori would never leave us alone.

Remi was the last to go. "Call if you need me during the night," he said, pointing to the house intercom near the door.

"I won't." Need him, that was. I wouldn't allow it. I spent years handling things on my own. I wasn't calling in backup to help me sleep at night.

Not that I'd be thinking about sleep if Remi were here during the night. All the more reason not to call.

Remi's jaw ticked in that way he had when there were things he wanted to say but wouldn't. Good.

"We'll talk more in the morning," he finally said.

I gave him a big smile and shut the door in his face.

The possibility of sleep was unlikely, but the nurse in me knew rest was essential if I wanted to think clearly, if I wanted to go after Brooke when the time came, so I went through as much of my nighttime ritual as I could, then crawled into the bed. On my side, a pillow hugged tight to my chest, I closed my eyes and forced some of my tension out with a hard sigh.

And another.

And...

I knew it was a dream the minute I saw Angelo's face. It was always Angelo in my dreams—the bad ones, at least. For the past year another face had invaded the good dreams, the sensual visions that snuck into my sleep. Remi's face. I knew I shouldn't think about him, dream about him, but found it impossible to stop.

This wasn't one of those dreams. I looked around at the pale walls, the brick of the old warehouse that had been converted to create the apartments Angelo had lived in on the farthest outskirts of DC. Our safe haven. The place he'd wanted me to share as his wife, with the extra room we'd planned to convert into a nursery.

Those walls were splashed with red. Angelo's blood. My blood.

My chest hurt, feeling like I'd run a hundred miles, my heaving breath doing nothing to fill the lungs in desperate need of air. Heavy cords bit into my skin, holding me down, the perfect target for every punch that came my way. And Angelo's eyes... They burned with anguish, with remorse. The most powerful man I'd ever known, helpless. The knowledge was killing him almost as surely as the blood loss stealing his strength.

"Look at this, John! We've got a pink room with a crib."

Bile rose to the back of my throat. Angelo had been so certain the baby was a girl. It had been too soon to know for sure, but he'd insisted on the pink. We hadn't had time to put the crib together yet.

We should've had time. All the time in the world. Now there was no more time.

"Stand her up," the man said, polishing the brass knuckles gleaming on his fingers. "He might not talk for her, but maybe he'll talk for it," he said, jerking his chin toward my slightly rounded stomach.

No. No no no no.

John undid the cord. I caught a glimpse of Angelo as I was jerked to my feet, and what I saw chilled my blood. Resignation. Fire. Grief. *I love you*, he mouthed. A tear wet the corner of his eye. *Take care of her.*

And then a mask descended over his face and he charged, chair and all. Joe and I were knocked off our feet by the impact.

I had to get away. I knew it, told my feet to move, stumbled around the breakfast bar to reach the apartment door—but all the while I braced myself for a grip on my shirt, dragging me back. A shout to stop or they'd fire. A gunshot sending agony through my body.

Only the last actually came, but it was Angelo who screamed in agony.

I shot upright in bed, that scream—the last sound I'd ever heard from the man I'd loved—mingling with my own. I couldn't tell which was real and which was a memory. Both echoed in my ears, the sound of a life being ripped apart.

And then the door to the room slammed open, bouncing off the wall to almost hit the man filling the doorway. "Leah?"

I brought my hand to my chest, fighting to slow my breathing, to bring my body back under control. To hide the things that made me vulnerable. "I'm all right."

"Like hell you're all right." Remi crossed the room to loom over the side of the bed, his silhouette blocking the light. "You were screaming like a banshee." He thrust his fingers through thick, messy hair. "Nightmare?"

I nodded, not wanting him to hear how hoarse my voice was. My throat felt like someone had sandpapered it. I knew from experience that I'd have that deep phone-sex quality to my voice for the next day or two. Too bad it wasn't sex that had caused it.

The sound of that gunshot, the remembered smell of heated blood came rushing back. A whimper escaped against my will.

"Fuck!"

The word sliced through the air, and then the covers were lifting and Remi's big body was crowding me back from the edge of the bed. "What are you doing?"

"Getting in. What's it look like?"

He wasn't wearing his shirt. I couldn't see much in the dim light of the room, but I didn't need to see; all I had to do was feel. I brought my hand up to ward Remi off—and met hard, hot flesh that pebbled with goose bumps beneath my fingers. Remi hesitated for barely a second, then used the bulk of his body to force me back onto the pillow.

Now both my hands were on his chest, and my heart was racing triple time for a whole different reason.

"Get out of my bed!"

I managed to keep the hysterical virgin out of my voice—I passed that stage a long time ago—but the indignant sex kitten came through loud and clear. Talk about mixed signals. I could read a five-page drug formulary in this voice and it would sound like a come-on. It also hurt like hell, so I shut my mouth and scrambled for the opposite side of the bed.

Remi's log of an arm blocked my retreat before I could escape. "Be still," he growled.

I was pulled firmly back until my spine hit his stomach, until the heat of his breath washed over my neck.

Until a solid rod nestled between the cheeks of my—

"Hey!"

Remi pushed his opposite arm beneath my neck, surrounding me, laying back a bit so I was forced to use his body as a pillow. "Hey, what?"

"Hey, *this*." I wiggled my butt against his erection.

Remi grunted as if I'd kicked him in the gut. "Ignore it. I am."

As if I could ignore a bat jutting into my backside. I mean, I'd seen Remi naked, but he'd been unconscious, relaxed. I knew he was built proportional to his body, but I hadn't expected this.

Maybe you're just out of practice.

Of course I was, but still…

Remi's broad palm flattened over my stomach, his heat seeping into me as he rubbed up to the underside of my breasts, then down to my pelvis. Up and down. Up and down. He was so warm.

God, it felt good. I could feel my muscles trying to relax, to give in, and I stiffened up again.

Remi's palm hesitated on my stomach. "I'm trying to comfort you, not rape you. Settle down."

Settle down? The words got my back up, but... Remi shifted, throwing a heavy thigh over both of mine. His hand took up its rhythm again. "I don't think you're trying to rape me," I said.

His thigh clenched, tightening around me. "Then why won't you be still?"

A huff escaped me, part irritation, part embarrassment. "Maybe because I'm too busy thinking about things I have no business thinking about?" I half yelled. Especially with him semi-naked and holding me down and— God, he really did feel good.

Remi went still, even his breath ceasing as he held me curled against him.

"At least I'm not thinking about nightmares," I muttered, a shudder working through me.

"Don't go believing I'm nice, Leah," he said, the words gruff in my ear.

"Right. You just rush into rooms with screaming women to, what, take advantage of them?" I shook my head. "You already denied that one. Relax, Remi. I won't make more of this than you do."

"Good." He shifted a bit, molding me closer to him until I could feel his heartbeat against my back. "Just doing the right thing."

Of course he was. I breathed in his scent—man and musk and something a little bit spicy—feeling it seep into the corners of my being. I firmly believed men like Remi were not to be trusted, but I also believed people weren't black-and-white. Remi hadn't kidnapped my child; he was trying to help get her back. He'd been stalking me, but now the intel he'd gathered could lead us to Brooke. He could be taking advantage of having me vulnerable in bed, but instead he was making me feel safer than I'd felt since those long-ago nights when Angelo had held me in his arms.

Angelo.

Remi went back to stroking my stomach. "Want to tell me about it?"

"About what?"

A chuckle tickled my ear. "You have to be the most contrary woman I've ever been this close to." He nipped the lobe, a sharp reprimand. "Your nightmare."

I shook my head. "Old memories."

"About Angelo's death?"

"Yes." But... "I should have known."

"Known what?"

"From the very beginning, Brooke has been seen as a pawn. That night..." I swallowed hard. "The men threatened to punch me in the stomach if he didn't talk. Until then, I think he'd thought he could get us out of this. He gave his life so I could escape with her." A shaky breath left me. "I've only ever wanted to protect her, but my choices keep finding her. Us. Again and again."

"Not your choices, Leah. His." Remi's hands clenched on my skin before easing off. "We're going to find her. We're going to stop the nightmares once and for all."

I rubbed my cheek over the rough hairs on the biceps beneath me. "Thank you."

Remi drew a deep breath, his chest pressing hard against me. "Sleep. Everything will be all right. I promise."

And even though I knew I shouldn't, I was starting to believe it was true. Remi would do everything he could to make it all right.

But then, so had Angelo.

Chapter Nine

Remi —

She'd finally fallen asleep in the early hours of the morning, curled in my arms. I couldn't seem to forget the warm scent of her, the feel of her, soft and strong all at once. I'd worked out for an hour in the gym, driving my body as hard as I could, desperate to think about anything, anyone else. My mind had basically flipped me the bird and kept on remembering.

Fucking bastard.

A quick, cold shower, then I made my way downstairs to the kitchen. None of us had to eat here. Each suite contained a small galley kitchen and eating area, but we'd been together so long it felt foreign to be apart. Every morning we found ourselves downstairs, gathered around the island. Being a family. Just the way my parents would've wanted it.

I wanted it that way too. Leah might not believe me, but I envied her. From the time I was little, all I had wanted was us together—my parents, Levi, Eli, me. Afternoons with milk and cookies, mornings huddled around the kitchen table—hell, even Saturday evenings spent trooping to the temple with yarmulkes on our heads. Being together had meant everything.

And then my uncle ripped us apart. Those first couple of years on the streets, I had held out hope that the three of us could build our own family, that someone we'd have a home again.

Twenty years later, we finally did. But those dreams of after-school snacks and presents under the tree?

There would be no kids in our future. What we did was too dangerous for that. It had hardened us too much.

"Where is my breakfast, bro?"

Eli stood next to the coffee maker, cup in hand, eyes still bleary from sleep. As the youngest he'd been protected in ways Levi and I couldn't afford for ourselves. Maybe that was why he slept at night.

"Fix it yourself, asshole." But I was already moving toward the fridge for eggs and bacon.

"I fixed the coffee," he protested.

"So pour me a cup and I'll consider making omelets for all of us." An onion and bell pepper waited in the crisper drawer. I pulled them out, along with the cheese, and started chopping.

Levi and Abby arrived minutes later, Abby taking over the bacon while I assembled omelets. Eli got off his ass long enough to throw some frozen biscuits in the oven. My culinary efforts didn't quite extend to homemade.

"How's Leah?" Abby asked quietly, her gaze on the crispy strips she was in charge of.

"Didn't sleep," I admitted.

"You don't look like you got much either."

Tipping my pan to peek under the eggs, see if they were done, I shrugged. I'd gone months without uninterrupted sleep before. As much as I told myself I shouldn't store up memories of Leah while she was here, those hours with her in my arms had been worth the fatigue. They were far more than I'd ever expected to have. Certainly far more than I deserved.

One omelet down, I passed the plate to Abby. "Levi, get up here and take over so your woman can eat."

Abby went to pass Levi with a cheeky grin, but my brother had other ideas. Circling her waist with an arm, he held her in place for a kiss that lasted until Eli began his "gross, get a room before I barf" routine. I could never admit it to anyone, but the open displays of affection made me uncomfortable too. Not in a teenage gross-out kind of way; more like I wanted to squirm, look away, get out of the same room with them, but at the same time I couldn't stop watching.

I didn't know why but suspected the instinct was in some way tied to those long-ago feelings I couldn't quite forget—family, affection.

For fuck's sake, I needed to get a grip. There were more important things to think about this morning.

I was finishing an omelet for Leah, ready to slip it into the oven to keep, when the phone in my pocket rang. Not my personal phone—that was on the counter where I could see it. This was Leah's phone, the one I'd swiped from her. The one only her brother had called in the past twenty-four hours.

I was calling for Abby even as I reached into my pocket. "Run get Leah. Hurry!"

Sure enough, the UNKNOWN caller was back. My brothers gathered around the island, all eyes on the screen, waiting for me to answer. Watching my back.

I laid the phone on the island, then clicked answer. The speakerphone filled the room...with silence.

"Hello, Windon," I said.

If he was surprised that I knew his name, he didn't let it slip. This man had lived a double life for a long time. It would take a lot to shake him.

My brothers and I were a whole fucking lot.

"Who are you?" he asked, ignoring my greeting.

"I'm not a helpless woman or child, I can tell you that." I let that sink in a moment. "I'm surprised, honestly. You come here to Atlanta, to my territory, and don't know who you're dealing with, who this area belongs to. You should've done your homework, cop."

Like we had. Windon was behind in the knowledge race, and now he knew it.

"Whoever you are, you obviously know my sister well."

"If you'd prepped, you'd have realized that before you made so many mistakes."

A harsh laugh filtered through the phone. "I have dealt with men far more dangerous than you, I am sure. Now let me talk to Leah."

"Not quite yet." I planted my fists on the counter. "Ever heard of the Assassin?"

A moment's hesitation. "You're not the Assassin."

So that was a yes.

Technically, I wasn't the assassin; Levi was. Or rather, he was the front man of our little operation. "No?" I asked silkily, letting him know how wrong he was. "Ask around. I think you'll find that you're wrong. If you can actually find me, that is."

"Listen to me, motherfucker," Windon growled. "This is between me and my sister. Whoever you are, you can fuck the hell off."

I leaned over the phone, letting menace drip from my words. "That's where you're wrong, *motherfucker*." I could feel my brother stares, feel them soaking in every word. "You waltzed into my town and messed with my woman, and it's not going to take me long to find you and make you regret every last breath you've ever taken."

A strangled sound came from the doorway to the kitchen. I didn't look up, didn't want to know what Leah felt about my words. She might never believe herself to be mine, but she was. Just because I couldn't have her didn't change how I felt.

The pad of bare feet crossing the room came to a stop next to me. I glared down at the phone. "Tell me where Brooke is and maybe I'll let you walk away with your life."

I heard Leah inhale, knew she was about to speak. Laying my hand over hers on the island, I squeezed. *Wait.*

She released her breath silently.

Trust. I swear my chest puffed up. And my brothers saw it, damn it. I could tell by Levi's wide eyes and Eli's smirk.

"I think I'll wait a little while longer," Windon said, his voice more confident than it should be. "In the meantime I think it might motivate my sister to hear her daughter's voice. Don't you think so, Leah?"

Leah's hand trembled beneath mine. "Yes."

She reached for the phone, but I held her back with a shake of my head. This should be a private moment and I wished I could give her that, but this might be our only chance to pick up clues. We needed to hear what Brooke said.

Leah's glare burned into me.

"Mommy?"

Her head whipped around to focus on the phone. "Brooke? Mommy is here, love. I'm right here."

"I'm ready to come home now. When will you pick me up?"

The little girl's voice was quiet, careful, much as I imagined Leah's had been as a child. Her past and her training might have helped hone her skills in a crisis, but her personality tended toward an introverted, quiet one. She'd fight tooth and nail where her daughter was concerned, but otherwise it was wait, see, evaluate. Brooke seemed to be the same.

"I know you want to be home, sweetheart," Leah was saying. "I want you there too. I'm trying to make it happen, I promise." She hesitated, fear flashing over her face. "Are you okay? You're not hurt, are you?"

"No. Mommy, Mrs. Lydia hurt her head. Is she okay? She couldn't come with me."

Leah dropped her elbows onto the island, her head into her hands. "She's…" Her fingers dug hard into her hair. "She's being looked at. Where are you—"

"I think that's enough," Windon said, cutting in. "We don't want to get Brooke too worked up." The man's tone turned thoughtful. "She reminds me so much of you, Leah. Always watching, always thinking. You were just like that."

Leah braced herself on the island. "You shut the fuck up about my daughter, Ross." Her breath hiccupped. "There were so many other ways you could've handled this, a hundred different approaches to take. You took the one that guaranteed I would never forgive you. Ever." She leaned close to the phone. "Do you remember what they did to Angelo that night? To me? Think about it hard, because I will make sure you suffer much, much worse."

My chest swelled even more.

"I don't have to think about it, Leah." Regret colored the words, but I refused to believe it. Leah was right; he could have handled this another way. "I remember every day, every second. I would've helped you then. I can help you now. Just give me the recordings."

"I can't give you what I don't have!"

"Then tell me where they are," Windon barked. "Tell me and let me get them and this will all go away."

"Will it?" Leah straightened, and I could see resignation in her eyes. "If you believe that, you've drunk more Kool-Aid than I ever thought possible."

"I'll tell you what I believe," Windon said. "Either I bring back those recordings, or I'm dead, Leah. My usefulness is at an end. It's this or nothing."

"So you led them right to me and my child? You knew!" she shouted. "You knew they would never let me walk away; I know too much! Or at least that's what they believe, but you brought them here anyway."

"I had no choice," Windon said. "Two days. That's all I have, all I can give you. In two days you'll have your daughter back. You know what I need to make that happen."

Leah started to answer, but I broke in. "Two days, Windon. Be ready."

Before he could respond, I clicked the call off.

"No!"

I caught Leah around the waist as she lunged for the cell. "He won't put her back on."

She struggled against me. "You don't know that!"

"I do." I dropped my chin onto the top of her head, wishing I could erase the longing, the pain in her voice. "But he gave us valuable information."

Leah stilled. "Like what?"

I turned to Eli. "Think you got enough to trace a location?"

Outrage pulled Eli back. "Is that even a question, bro?" Picking up the cell, he jerked his head toward the elevator. "Give me a few and I'll have what you need."

Leah stared after him. I stared at her.

Levi cleared his throat. When I glanced his way, he raised an eyebrow.

I nodded in response. "Let's fix you a plate," I told Leah. "Then I'll show you the bat cave."

Chapter Ten

Leah —

"Bat cave, really?"

Remi threw a grin I could only describe as sheepish over his shoulder as he led me out of the elevator. "What else would we call it?"

"An office?" Did assassins have offices? But as I looked around the massive basement, I knew he was right—this could only be called a bat cave.

Equipment was stacked everywhere, the walls lined with so many screens and monitors that the light paint could barely be seen. It looked like they needed a secretary. Or housemaid. The only thing missing was a massive glass case with the Batman suit in it, which I didn't see. I did see a corner with a couch and a huge mass of video gaming equipment.

Guess they had to blow off steam somehow.

Eli sat at a station about halfway down the room, eating absently, his gaze locked on the screens in front of him. As we got closer, I realized he was watching traffic footage.

"Find anything?" Remi pulled out a rolling chair next to his brother and gestured for me to sit. After hearing Brooke's voice, my restlessness had ratcheted up exponentially, but standing meant I was farther from the screens. I sat.

"Thank you." I shot Remi a grateful smile.

A warm, massive hand landed on my shoulder. Remi gave me a squeeze.

"I managed to triangulate their location," Eli was saying, either missing the byplay or ignoring it like I wished I could ignore Remi's touch. "A grocery store parking lot on the west side of town. Too public to be a permanent location." Eli clicked on an image of a car at the far, isolated end of a megamart lot. When he zoomed in, I could make out Ross's face, but Brooke was no more than a vague, pale shadow between the driver's and passenger's seats.

"Could they be staying somewhere in the area?" I asked, swallowing back my disappointment.

"Unlikely." Eli pointed to the top screen that showed heavy traffic on I285. "They're good. They know where the cameras will follow them and where they won't. They drove around a bit, got off the freeway, and disappeared."

"Same routine they pulled when they left Leah's house," Remi said.

They'd tried to track Ross from my house?

"Yep," Eli agreed. "Windon and his associate know how to stay out of sight."

I glanced at the still image showing the car in the parking lot. Ross sat in the passenger's seat, his arm extended as he held the phone to Brooke's face. Beside him, in the driver's seat, sat another man. I couldn't make out much more than dark clothes and hair. It could be anyone.

"Who is the second man?" I asked.

Eli did some quick clicking, and a mug shot appeared on one of the unused screens. "Name is Joe Southerland. Been in jail multiple times for crimes believed to be tied to the Fiori mob family."

My heart jumped into my throat. "What kind of crimes?"

Remi squeezed my shoulder again, his thumb drifting to the back of my neck. "You don't want to know that."

"He's obviously loyal to the family," Eli put in. "Fiori is making sure Ross stays put, is my guess."

"We know they're blackmailing him," Remi said.

I flinched. Much as I hated Ross right now, he was my brother. Older than me, yes, but my childhood had been full of memories of the two of us. Good memories. It was hard to believe the man I knew had become a mob informant and Lord only knew what else. Had he "lost" evidence? Misled investigations? Passed on faulty information? Had he killed for them?

The thought made my stomach cramp.

"The problem is"—Remi straightened, came around Eli's chair to lean back against the desk—"too much pressure on a guy this far out on a limb and he's likely to snap."

I rubbed at the ache beginning between my eyes. God, please don't let Ross snap with Brooke in his possession.

"So what's our plan? What do we do?" I asked.

Remi slid his knuckles back and forth over the stubble on his cheek. "We don't have a location, no leads at this point. Right now our only option is to meet Windon in two days like he wants."

"What?" The tripping of my heartbeat pushed me to my feet. "We can't wait that long!"

"We don't have an alternative." The words were implacable, but the sympathy in Remi's expression told me he had some idea how hard they were to swallow.

Eli swiveled his seat around. "I won't stop looking, Leah. I have a program running right now, searching all camera feeds for the last two days for that license plate, the make and model of the car, everything. If I get even a whiff, you'll hear about it."

"And if we can find her, we'll go in sooner," Remi said. "Until then our best bet is to find the recordings."

That ache shifted to the back of my skull. Why would no one believe me? "I don't know where they are."

"You never know what you don't know till you find it."

"That makes no sense," I told Eli. Actually it made perfect sense. I just wanted to be contrary. Why? Because everything in my life was out of my control, I'd failed at the most important job I'd ever had, and Remi was looking at me with that damn sympathy in his eyes again.

"Have a seat, Leah."

I narrowed my eyes at him. "I'd rather stand." If I confined myself in a chair again, I might start screaming and never stop.

He didn't argue. He stared me down. "You can do this, Leah. Have a seat so we can see the intel Eli has pulled."

I glanced down at Eli's blond head, studiously down to avoid our fighting. On the screen directly in front of him was what looked like multiple documents, including a mug shot of Angelo when he was much, much younger than when I'd known him.

Biting my lip, I sat in the chair and scooted closer to Eli. "Okay."

"I've got what little was public record," Eli said, a hint of amusement in his voice before he cleared it. "And some of what wasn't. Looks like Angelo stayed pretty far under the radar."

Remi crossed his legs at the ankles. "Unusual for an enforcer. Usually they can't contain the rage."

Angelo hadn't seemed angry. He'd just seemed...normal. Sure, on the dangerous side, dominant, but not in a threatening way. At least not toward me.

"A couple of scrapes in juvie, but that's about it," Eli was saying. "Not even a speeding ticket. Nothing until the investigation into his death."

Remi leaned over to eye the screen. "An investigation that went nowhere."

That didn't surprise me. Ross could even have been the one to somehow block the investigation.

Eli clicked through the case file. I didn't know how he'd gotten ahold of it, but nothing the brothers did really surprised me anymore. When Eli got to the autopsy report and photos, I hastily looked away.

Right into Remi's eyes.

It hit me like a lightning bolt every time that happened. Our eyes would meet, and something electric would pass between us, something so strong it scared me. I'd felt it the first time he opened his eyes from the coma, and every time after until Levi had set me free. And I'd tried to forget. But with him right in front of me, with that electricity sizzling in the air between us...

Did it bother him to hear about Angelo? I'd certainly never imagined Remi with other women, but that wasn't realistic, was it? This man was no longer an invalid, and there had to have been women.

And you have a child. If it hurts him, tough shit. We need this info to get Brooke back.

"No mention of mob activity, previous dealings with Fiori or the mob." Out of the corner of my eye I saw Eli click the file closed, and I turned to face the computer again. "It was assumed it was a random robbery gone wrong because of the state of the house. Cold case, unsolved."

"They searched that night," Remi said.

"Everywhere." I stared down at my hands clasped on the desk, my white knuckles. "If something had been there, surely they'd have found it."

"Did Angelo have a secret hiding place?"

I dug my nails into my palms, trying to contain the memories. "Not that I know of, but I wasn't living there. We talked about it, but…" My throat closed up.

"What about outside of the house? Safety deposit box, favorite place to visit, anything like that?"

"I don't know about a box. We walked to his cousin's Italian restaurant every couple of days." Angelo had loved food as much as I had back then, before caring for a child and lack of time had made me more cautious. "That was our only regular hangout."

Remi grunted, the rasp of his thumb tracing his stubble a harsh complement. "Did he ever give you anything?"

"All the time." Most of it had been left behind, but… "Angelo liked to give me things—food, clothes, books."

"Any jewelry?" Eli asked.

I shuddered, the memories flooding over the dam I'd built to keep them back. "He...he gave me a ring that night. An engagement ring. But...they took it, before they...started..." A wave of my hand filled in what I couldn't get my tongue to explain. "You know."

I brought a hand to my lips, holding back words and emotion I had no desire to share.

"Eli"—Remi straightened—"give us a minute?"

I didn't look up, didn't want to see what Eli thought of me, of my past. And God, I didn't want to see sympathy. Pity. I'd lost a lot, yes, but I had gotten through it. That was my focus, not—

A hand appeared in front of my eyes. "C'mere."

The fingers were thick, strong. They looked like they could weather any storm, and probably could. But when this was over, there'd be no hand to grab hold of. I wouldn't let there be.

But right now? I needed that hand. So I took it.

Chapter Eleven

Remi —

My basic philosophy in life, given my past, was *shit happens*. I deserved it. Leah didn't.

Clients didn't tell us why they wanted a hit; they just paid us. It was up to us to find out the why, to decide if it was a job worth taking. I had read some messed-up shit in my time, but it had never affected me the way Leah's simple "you know" did.

The look in her eyes... Fuck.

"C'mere," I said, needing to touch her, to feel her body against me and know in that moment that she was safe. Whole.

She stared at my hand for a long moment, and I braced myself for her rejection. Held my breath. The moment her fingers slipped into mine and she rose from her chair, I knew I didn't deserve it.

I took it anyway.

Shifting my legs apart, I pulled her close until her belly met my groin and her breasts plumped against my chest. The sensation was almost indescribable—like coming home and getting hit with a jolt of electricity all at once. Leah's head fit right in the hollow of my shoulder, and as she settled there, her deep sigh echoed my own.

Home.

She drew in a breath, pressing her breasts harder against me.

Electricity.

Fuck.

"I don't need your sympathy, Remi," she said, her voice not as certain as her words.

I ran my palms up her back, down along the dip of her spine. "Who said it was sympathy?"

"Okay then." She shifted, her body molding even closer to mine. A groan caught in the back of my throat. "I don't need to be cuddled."

"Maybe I need it," I said, not bothering to hide the hoarse tone creeping in. If we could have nothing else between us, there needed to be truth. I wanted her body, no doubt about it, but I'd give anything to take care of her. To love her.

She went rigid against me, the ease of her body against mine gone in a hot second. "Why would you need it?"

"Why do you think?"

Stepping back, Leah narrowed her eyes. "This isn't about sex."

Tell my dick that. If her body was against mine, there would always be an undercurrent of hunger beneath whatever else was going on between us; that was fact. "It isn't *all* about sex."

"No." Panic filtered into her eyes as they landed everywhere but where I needed them to be—on me. "Absolutely not."

I crossed my arms over my chest and simply looked at her. We both knew the truth, whether she wanted to admit it or not.

Both fists tightened at her sides. "So I tell you about the worst night of my life and you want to fuck, is that it?"

The words hit their mark, deadlier than an armor-piercing round. Leah had known just where to strike.

Weaknesses aren't allowed, remember?

So why did it feel like she'd just cut out my heart?

Straightening, I shoved myself away from the desk. "Let's head upstairs."

I was halfway across the room before I realized Leah wasn't following. I didn't want to care. Before this woman, I'd avoided caring about anyone but my brothers. Somehow she broke through the barriers I'd never allowed to be breached, found the soft underbelly I hadn't known existed.

Fuck that.

"Remi."

My name on her lips jerked my body to a stop without my permission. How the hell had I let a woman I'd had no more than a handful of conversations with gain this kind of power over me? Planting my hands on my hips, I glared up at the ceiling and wished I could just keep walking. "Yeah?"

Footsteps behind me, soft, suspicious—a barefoot attacker, knife ready to slip between my ribs. She stopped just out of sight. "I'm sorry."

Was she? She'd gotten what she wanted—me away from her.

"I just— I don't understand what's going on here."

Who the fuck did? "We're trying to find your daughter, Leah. That's it." The fact that my heart hadn't got the fucking memo didn't mean a damn thing.

"No, that's not it, and you know it." She walked around to face me. "I mean what's going on between us. What's— " She swallowed hard, her gaze drifting from mine again. "Why were you following me?"

I'd have thought that was obvious. "Apparently I was looking for the first chance to sweep in and force you to fuck me."

Leah flinched. Her arms crossed over her ribs, gripping tight. "I guess I deserve that."

I didn't answer, wouldn't allow myself to strike out any more than I already had.

"Remi…" Shoving a hand through her hair, Leah raised her eyes to mine. "I am sorry I said that. I know it's not true."

I forced my tense muscles to soften, forced my anger away. Tearing each other apart wouldn't get us anywhere; the only thing that would was clearing away the bullshit.

"You were protecting yourself."

A strained chuckle left her. "From what?"

"From the fact that you want me."

A flush of pink crept across her cheeks. "No, I don't. I—"

I was just enough of a bastard not to let that one pass. "Do you really want me to prove it?" I asked, one eyebrow arched.

The panic that had sparked this whole shit show made a hasty return. Of course she didn't want me to prove it. Then she might have to admit she lusted after a killer.

That's what I was, what I would always be in her eyes. I'd accepted it a long time ago. It was only when I looked into those fierce brown eyes that I wanted to be something different.

"Remi, we can't— I don't—"

"You don't?" I stepped forward, something in me relishing Leah's sudden retreat. "We can't?" If I was the bad guy, why not own it? Give in? Prove to us both that I wasn't worthy to touch the princess. To have her.

I might not be worthy, but that didn't mean I wasn't fully capable.

"Remi."

"Jeremiah," I barked, unable to resist the constant need to hear my full name on her lips. This might be my only opportunity.

"Jer—what?"

"My name," I said, gravel coming to the fore. "Jeremiah." Levi, Jeremiah, Elijah. Our heritage was strong, and we carried it with us despite the fact that our parents had been ripped away. "Jeremiah."

Leah's step hitched. Her lips curved, forming the first syllable of my name.

"Say it." I prowled closer. "Say it, Leah."

Her back hit the wall behind her. She startled, shook her head.

I planted my fists on either side of her shoulders and leaned close. "Why not? Too intimate?" I nuzzled her ear, taking in her scent like the animal I'd become, the animal I kept tightly under control. "What are you afraid I'll hear if you say my name?"

"I'm not afraid."

The trembling in her words said otherwise. Something deep inside me purred at the realization.

Christ, what was wrong with me?

"Tell me, Leah." I trailed my lips over the shell of her ear. Took the lobe between my teeth and nipped. "It's been a year and a half. Are you telling me there wasn't a single night in all that time that you didn't dream of me? Didn't wake up in the middle of the night and touch yourself, imagining it was my fingers, my mouth. My cock."

A small sound escaped her.

This time I nipped the curve of her jaw.

"Tell me," I said again. "Tell me you haven't wanted me every day for the last eighteen months just like I've wanted you. Tell me you haven't thought about me. Tell me you didn't care if you never saw me again." I skated my lips along the velvet curve of her jawline. "Say my name, Leah. Say it and I'll let you go."

It was a lie. This close to kissing her? I could never let her go. Pulling back might destroy me.

I licked the corner of her mouth. "Say it."

Her lips opened, so slowly. She turned until our mouths lined up, allowing me to see the hesitant desire in her eyes even while her body remained tense. "Jeremiah."

I groaned, swallowing my name on her lips. But it was Leah who raised just that little bit onto her tiptoes and took my mouth with hers.

I was lost the minute her mouth opened against mine.

Coffee and Leah and truth. That's what I tasted. Maybe this was the only truth we could have between us, with our bodies. The place where what we told ourselves and each other dissolved and what we truly felt came through. I'd never wanted that with anyone else, but with Leah I craved that shit like a drug.

Reaching down, I grasped behind her knees and lifted, urged her to hook her legs around my waist. Leah's hands fisted in my T-shirt; my weight pressed her into the wall. The position opened her body to me, my cock fitting as natural as breathing into the notch between her legs. I licked into her mouth, pressed my lips hard against the softness of hers. Ground my erection against her body.

A surprised sound filtered from her mouth to mine. I swallowed it down.

She felt like a fucking dream, and maybe that's what she was. How many times had I imagined this moment, imagined thrusting my tongue into her mouth, tangling with hers, swallowing the taste of her over and over. How many times had I imagined the tightness of her nipples dragging against my chest, the damp heat of her pussy against my cock? More times than I could count. More often than I'd admit even to myself, but here it was, finally. Absolutely.

Jeremiah.

My cock kicked against Leah's clit.

She dragged her mouth away, but her hands were in my hair, digging deep, refusing to let me escape. I bent to her neck, took the skin between my teeth and sucked hard, needing my mark on her, needing to brand her as mine. Needing to prove this moment was real and I wasn't about to wake up with come splashed across my belly like I had a million times before.

"Remi." Leah panted in my ear. Her hips rolled against mine, threatening to undo me. "God, Remi!"

So close. She'd been in my arms less than five minutes, and she was so close to climax. I could hear it in her voice, feel it in the urgency of her pelvis as she rode the ridge of my cock. And I wanted to give it to her more than I'd ever wanted anything in my life, including my own release. I wanted to see her body seize, see the tension ball up and explode, leaving her soft and pliant in my arms.

Snaking a hand beneath her T-shirt, I smoothed over hot skin until I found the edge of her bra. Shoved up. Taking Leah's mouth again, I plumped her breast and pinched the taut nipple between my fingers.

Leah surged against me. A high whine escaped into my mouth.

I pinched again, rolled the tip between finger and thumb.

She convulsed in my arms.

Pressing her hard into the wall, I let her ride my cock as she hit her peak. Swallowed every moan and sob as each wave took her. Eyes open, I soaked in the beauty of orgasm on her face, the strain and need and, finally, relief. I soaked it in and knew this was far more than I'd ever deserved. Leah's trust, her vulnerability.

The greatest gift I'd ever been given.

And when she tipped her head back against the wall, trying to breathe, trying to regain control, I buried my face in the curve of her neck and wished I could keep her forever. It was fucking stupid, a child's impossible dream, to become someone else, someone worthy of the only woman I'd ever wanted to possess. But I closed my eyes and prayed to whatever force might be listening to somehow, please, make it come true.

Chapter Twelve

Leah —

My mind was a mix of haze and satisfaction. Surrounded by Remi's warmth and strength, I floated on a sea of nothingness that I never wanted to leave. And Remi's head tucked against my neck— I'd never associated tenderness with my feelings for this man, but right now, with his head bowed against me and his arms holding me up… My heart melted.

I released the handfuls of shirt fisted in my fingers and slid them up the smooth expanse of his neck to the tendrils of hair that were just long enough to curl. His breath hitched at my touch, his hips shifting the slightest bit between my legs.

He was hard. Still hard, his heart drumming against my breast.

He hadn't come.

"Remi."

He growled against my throat, the vibrations sending aftershocks through my body.

"Jeremiah," I said softly, the syllables spilling from my tongue with a sweet ache I hadn't intended to reveal.

This time Remi purred.

"I—" My knees clenched involuntarily, nudging him closer. "You haven't—"

The swish of the elevator doors opening cut off whatever I'd been struggling to say.

"Wow!" Eli crossed the room, one hand coming up to block his view of us against the wall. Of course his fingers were parted, so it wasn't very effective. Perv. "Not what I thought I'd be interrupting, but okay."

A warning rumbled against my shoulder. "Dickhead."

I choked back a laugh. Then groaned as Remi backed up and allowed my legs to slide from his hips.

I hadn't used those muscles in a while. Ouch.

I'd definitely used them with Remi. The fact that the thought didn't send me into a tailspin of panic should have set off warning sirens in my brain, but there were too many endorphins already swimming around in there for it to make much headway.

Remi's big hands were on my hips, rubbing discreetly along the joints and the tops of my thighs as if he knew exactly what I was feeling. I slid my palms down to his biceps, gripping the heavy muscles until his eyes met mine.

"I—"

Damn. Why was I always fumbling with words with this man?

Remi's lips were tight, his body tense. Guilt hammered at me. Was he upset that I had finished and he hadn't? Was he wishing this hadn't happened? Was he—

He leaned in until his lips brushed my ear. "Damn my little brother and his fucking interruptions," he growled. And it was a growl—the words quaked through my body, sending shards of pleasure to places that really shouldn't be feeling this way with someone else in the room with us.

A little hiccup of a laugh escaped me.

Remi straightened, cleared his throat. "Let's get out of here."

My heart leaped in my chest. Did he— Were we—

Damn words.

The truth was, whatever had happened against that wall, I wasn't ready to go to bed with Remi. I wanted to; I couldn't deny that, not now. But…

What was I thinking? This wasn't why I was here. And Remi wasn't the kind of man I should have a sexual relationship with. The kind of man I should bring into my daughter's life. Was he?

"Relax," he said, and I glanced up to meet his knowing gaze. "I'm not gonna throw you over my shoulder and haul you off to the nearest bed, Leah."

"Why not?" Eli asked from across the room.

"Shut the fuck up, asshole," Remi barked.

God, I needed to get out of here before the blushes consumed me and all that was left was a pile of ash.

"Come on," Remi said, taking my elbow. I couldn't help but notice that his first couple of steps were stiff, awkward. Guilt spiked again. "We're out," he called as he escorted me to the elevator.

I resisted. "But shouldn't we—"

"No worries, sweetheart," Eli said over his shoulder, ignoring Remi's muttering at the endearment. "Everything is pretty much on automatic right now, but I'm still digging. If I find anything else, you'll be the first to know."

I looked to Remi, who nodded. I let him pull me into the elevator. Remi hit the button for the third floor.

I cleared my throat.

The door slid open.

Remi glanced at the thick black watch on his wrist as we exited. "I have something I need to take care of. You'll be all right for a few hours? Eli will make sure you're kept informed."

Disappointment stirred in my stomach.

"Eli will, but what about you?" I asked. "I want my phone." I needed that connection to Brooke, however nebulous.

"I don't think that's a good idea."

All those lovely endorphins did a rapid disappearing act. "It doesn't matter what you think, Remi. I want my phone."

"Lea—"

"Don't!" I planted my hands on my hips. "If you can't trust that I'm going to stay put, that I recognize you are my best bet of getting my daughter back, then…" Honestly, I didn't know what. All I knew was I needed this.

"It's not about trusting you," he said.

"Yes, it is. Either you think I'll stay, or you think I'll run." *And whatever happened downstairs meant nothing.* Was that what he was telling himself? Because after those moments in his arms, I could no longer deny what I knew was the truth—there was something between us. Where it would lead? Who the hell knew.

Remi stared at me for so long I thought he'd flat-out refuse. Until his hand slid into his pocket and he drew out my phone.

"Come find one of us if anything happens, got it? My number is programmed into your phone. Call immediately," he said.

I grasped the only lifeline I had to my daughter. "Immediately," I agreed.

Remi nodded. He turned, hesitated, turned back. "I won't be gone long."

The reassurance settled something uncertain inside me. "Okay."

"Okay." He disappeared into his room.

Too restless to be confined to my bedroom again, I wandered downstairs. My mind raced, wondering how I'd fill hours of waiting, of doing nothing while Brooke was somewhere out there, missing me, wishing she was home. The longing to see her, hold her and know she was safe was killing me.

Yes, even when I had been in Remi's arms, she hadn't been far from my thoughts.

Except there at the end.

Well, yeah. I rolled my eyes at myself. I wasn't one of those moms who thought I couldn't have something for myself apart from my daughter; I was too practical for that. The nurse in me, probably. I just never had, but that was more lack of desire than anything else. Still, I couldn't deny the hint of guilt knowing Brooke was alone and I had…what? Taken comfort from Remi? Relief? I didn't know what to call it, and right now I didn't care.

I reached the foyer just as Abby entered from the direction of the kitchen. She shot me an understanding glance. "Restless?"

Abby, probably more than anyone, understood my position, I was sure. "Limbo sucks."

"To put it mildly." She gestured toward the front door. "I have just the distraction."

The massive door opened smoothly to Abby's touch. I followed her outside as a black Expedition with darkly tinted windows pulled to a stop at the bottom of the stairs. The driver's side door opened, and a man I could only describe as a Viking stepped out. Tall, blonde, muscular. A bit more polished than his Nordic ancestors, but it only took one look into those piercing blue eyes to see the warrior the business suit he wore did a lousy job of hiding.

The man rounded the vehicle and opened the passenger door for a petite woman who exited slowly, carefully, her long, dark hair hiding her face. Abby squealed and rushed toward her. The Viking's eyes narrowed, his mouth tensing. Just before he jumped in front of her, Abby slowed, coming up against the woman gently for a hug.

"Charlotte." She stepped back, eyeing the woman. "How are you? Healing okay?"

I couldn't hear the woman's response; her voice was soft, almost as gentle as the hug Abby had given her. What wasn't gentle was the Viking's searing gaze as it transferred from Abby and the woman to me where I stood at the top of the stairs. I didn't miss the step closer to his charge, the way his arm came up to pull her close, shelter her against his side.

Either the man was in the same business as Remi and his brothers, or something very close. That eagle look in his eyes, the body built like a brick wall—he had *dangerous* written all over him.

Abby moved to Charlotte's other side, gesturing the couple up the steps. "Leah." A bright smile lit her face. "Let me introduce you to my good friend, Charlotte Alexander. Charlotte, our…houseguest, Leah Marrone."

Nice save. I moved to shake the woman's extended hand, keeping a sharp eye on the Viking's tense muscles. "Nice to meet you."

"And you, Leah," Charlotte said, her voice both formal and warm at the same time. "This is my fiancé, King Moncrief."

A large hand with long, elegant fingers came my way.

"Of course," I said, shaking the man's hand. "It had to be either Viking or royalty; I wasn't sure which."

One side of King's mouth turned up. Charlotte's rich laugh pealed out between us.

"She does have you pegged," Abby said, smirking. "You have to admit."

"I admit nothing," the blond god said, eyes lightening with amusement. He gathered Charlotte close once more and urged her toward the door. "Where is your other half?"

"Right here." Levi was descending the staircase as we entered the house. I'd never seen the man in person in anything but T-shirts and fatigues, but now—holy cow. The suit he wore fit him like it had been molded to his body, the fabric smoothing over his muscles like silk. But if he looked delicious, the man descending behind him was a gourmet meal ten times over. Remi was taller and broader than his brother, and the navy-blue fabric of his suit set off his coloring to perfection, somehow soothing his ragged edges while enhancing the power his big body naturally projected. Where Levi wore a silk tie, Remi had left his white dress shirt open at the throat, the vee of darker skin making me want to bury my face there and taste the rough texture, nip at the hard edges of his collarbone.

I squeezed my thighs together as unobtrusively as I could. Remi's eyebrow arched, and I knew he'd caught the gesture.

Beautiful bastard.

"We won't be gone long," Levi was telling Abby when I was finally able to notice anything but Remi. "Eli's downstairs."

"I expect you to rest," King said to Charlotte. "And call me if you need anything."

Charlotte cupped his face, her look indulgent. "I won't lift a finger, promise."

"I won't let her," Abby chimed in.

"Better not," the Viking growled before leaning down to give his fiancée a kiss that sent a blush burning across my cheeks.

Levi nudged Abby back from the crowd, his broad shoulders blocking any view of his goodbye to her. That left Remi and me standing awkwardly alone. Did the other couples' open affection make him as uncomfortable as it did me? Would he march out the door without a goodbye?

Did I want him to?

Remi moved into my space until I couldn't see anyone but him. "A couple of hours. If you hear anything, have Eli call me. Promise."

Not a question, a demand. And yet it soothed me instead of irritating me. Remi was as concerned about Brooke as I was.

"Promise," I said.

Without warning Remi reached up to grasp my chin, holding me steady for a quick, hard kiss. "Back soon," he muttered, and then he was gone, leaving me standing in the middle of the foyer with a stuttering heart and confusion clouding my brain.

Chapter Thirteen

Leah —

Abby brought tea to a room at the back of the house that I hadn't seen yet, a library. The long, soft couch was the perfect place for Charlotte to put her feet up. I helped her settle while Abby set up the refreshments.

"Do you mind me asking about your injury?" I gave her midriff a nod. "I'm a nurse."

Charlotte gave me the soft smile that I was quickly coming to associate with her. "Knowing that might've made King easier about leaving me."

"He's as territorial as Levi," Abby put in.

"Especially now. I was shot," she explained as casually as if she were discussing an ice cream sundae.

My gaze jumped to Abby's, my heart speeding up at the thought of this tiny woman in front of a gun. I'd thought King was dangerous; had he brought a threat into Charlotte's life? Was he more like Levi than I'd thought?

Seeming to sense my rising anger—and its focus—Abby stepped in quickly to place a pillow behind her friend's back. "Charlotte's fiancé works for JCL Securities, the largest security firm in the nation," she said.

Oddly enough, I'd actually heard of them. A few years ago one of the founding partner's girlfriends had been stalked by a psycho ex and then kidnapped.

They'd later discovered the man was a serial murderer. The whole episode had made headlines.

So King was a legit killer instead of a criminal one?

"This had nothing to do with King's job, though," Charlotte was saying.

"So how did it happen?"

Charlotte waved her hand as if the *how* didn't matter, although the lurking shadows in her eyes said differently. "It's a really long story. What gets me is that King took the same bullet—I was standing in front of him—and he barely acts like he's hurt. I think he's just faking it."

No doubt his injuries, based on his body weight and the fact that he'd gotten a less severe impact, weren't as extensive as Charlotte's. I'd seen plenty of gunshot wounds in my time and knew how much damage they could do to such a petite body.

"A man like him wouldn't want to admit a weakness."

"See?" Abby passed Charlotte a teacup. "I told you. Even Leah knows, these badass men want us to believe they are invincible."

A memory of Angelo the last time I saw him, moments before his death, flashed in my mind. "No one is invincible."

"That's what I told him," Charlotte complained. "It managed to keep him home with me for the first couple of weeks, but now..."

"I doubt it was anything you said," I told her, a smirk tugging at my lips. I might not know King personally, but I knew his type. "He just didn't want you out of his sight."

"Right?" Abby handed my tea across, gesturing to a nearby seat. "All it takes is one gun in your face or your house burning down, and the next thing you know, they go all Neanderthal on your ass."

Outrage mixed with indulgence on Charlotte's and Abby's faces, telling me they didn't mind as much as they might let on.

"I think the light duty is getting on his nerves," Charlotte said after a sip of her drink. "He's ready to get back to his team. He volunteered to help get this new team installed at Hacr, but as much as he doesn't mind administration, he wants off desk duty and back in action."

Abby was nodding as if she completely understood. No doubt she did. I couldn't see Levi being content with "desk duty." Those few days when Remi had been unconscious, Levi had been like a bear with a sore paw tied to a telephone pole. Any action was better than waiting.

Exactly how I felt right now.

"So how do you know each other?" I asked, sitting back in my seat. This felt good. I couldn't remember the last time I'd sat around and chatted with other women outside of work. Hospitals were the biggest gossip rings around, but who was sleeping with whom and who was about to get themselves fired didn't exactly interest me. I'd been too focused on Brooke and—

You should be focused on her now too.

The guilt hit me broadside, followed by a frustration chaser. For a few moments I'd forgotten how helpless I was in this situation.

"We've known each other for years," Abby was saying. "But we really only connected recently."

The shadows reappeared in Charlotte's eyes. "The price of being raised in wealthy, influential families. Nothing seems to matter but them." She flashed a bright smile Abby's way. "But we made it despite them, didn't we?"

"We did."

Abby had been forced to shoot her father shortly after I'd been released. He'd tried to kill her, the official story said, after she discovered evidence that he'd had her birth mother murdered. With family like that, maybe being with Levi didn't seem all that foreign to her. The man might be a killer, but no one could deny the authenticity of his feelings for Abby.

Knowing Abby's history made me all the more curious about Charlotte's story.

"So, Leah, what about you?" Charlotte asked.

I shook away my thoughts. "What about me?"

Abby smirked, a knowing look in her eyes. "That was a very interesting goodbye Remi gave you earlier."

I choked on the swallow of tea I'd just taken.

"Remi, huh?" Charlotte grinned. "He's a handsome one."

"Handsome." Abby nodded. "And big." One eyebrow arched.

You have no idea. The visceral memory of him between my legs, of exactly how *big* he was, sent heat rushing to places I really didn't want to think about right now.

"Look at that blush!" Abby threw back her head, her laughter filling the room. "We must know all!"

"Dish, girl," Charlotte said teasingly.

"I—" Oh boy. I didn't want to talk about this. "There's nothing between me and Remi."

"That's not what Eli told me," Abby said.

I groaned. Charlotte snorted. "He gossips more than a gaggle of women in a hair salon."

I dropped my head into my hands. I didn't even want to know...

"You know, if you don't tell details," Charlotte said, "that just means we get to speculate more."

"And isn't that fun?" Abby laughed.

Oh hell.

I peeked up from my hand, then straightened, giving them both a little smile. "I'm just...uh..." I shook my head. Did I really want to admit this out loud? "I don't think Remi and I are the best idea," I said, throwing Abby a significant look. She of all people should understand why I felt that way.

A sympathetic look said she did.

Charlotte was nodding too. "I thought that for a long time with King." She eased forward to settle her cup on the low table between us, then eased back to the cushions with a sigh. "Stupid gunshot," she muttered, voice husky with pain. "We go way back, King and I. But for the longest time I thought we weren't good for each other. Or he thought we weren't." She shrugged carefully. "Sometimes what you thought you wanted is what kept you dead inside all along. Only taking a chance can change that. It was a lesson we had to learn together."

I stared into my now lukewarm tea as Charlotte's words sank into my heart. Was that really what this was? A chance to come alive? I'd been trudging along for so many years, treading water, Brooke the only real light in my life. Earlier, in Remi's arms, I'd felt more alive than I had since Angelo's death.

But was it worth it? When this was over, Remi would be gone. Did I want to feel alive now, only to go back to feeling numb? If I was lucky. Men like Angelo and Remi brought just as much pain as joy into your life. After Angelo had been killed, I'd wanted to die with him. Only the child growing inside me had kept me going. And now…

Thoughts whirled in my head as Abby and Charlotte moved on to talk about an upcoming charity event. It was a bit surreal, hearing them discuss thousand-dollar-a-plate dinners when, just downstairs, an assassins' lair waited. Upstairs was civility; downstairs was danger, which only underscored the conflict in my own mind.

A conflict that got shoved aside when the phone in my pocket buzzed.

I jumped a good foot, like someone had goosed me in the ass. Abby frowned my way.

"I have to—" I fumbled the phone out of my jeans. "Please excuse me." A glance told me the caller was a fellow nurse from work, Meredith. "I'll be right back."

Hurrying from the room, I put the phone to my ear. "Hey, Meredith."

"Hello, my dear." The cultured greeting was typical of Meredith. An older nurse with a vast reserve of both knowledge and patience, she never lost her manners, her compassion, or her calm.

So why did she sound on the verge of frazzled?

"Is everything all right?" I asked carefully. It wasn't unusual for us to chat at lunch or call each other on an off day, but her voice…

No, this wasn't a casual phone call.

"Honestly, no. Or rather, I'm not sure. It could be nothing…"

"It's all right." *Just tell me!* "What's up?"

"Your locker here at work was broken into."

My feet were already rushing for the elevator. "My locker?"

"Yes." The sound of people talking came and went. "I was getting off shift, and as I went to leave, I noticed the bolt was broken on your lock. Security hasn't found anything, and I can't tell if anything is missing."

Likely nothing since I never kept more than a change of clothes in there when I wasn't on duty.

"I was hoping you could come in, check the contents?"

The elevator doors opened in the basement. Eli swiveled to face me as I rushed across the room.

"Actually, Meredith, I'm—" Where was I? What excuse could I come up with? "I'm out of town with Brooke for a little girl time this weekend."

Eli raised an eyebrow. I could practically see the wheels turning as he worked to put the pieces together from only one side of the discussion.

"I don't think I can get back until my next shift. Would you be willing to take my things out of my locker and take them home with you? I can pick them up from you Monday." Maybe.

"Aren't you worried something might be missing?"

"If my change of clothes and the picture of Brooke are still there, nothing was taken."

A pause. "The clothes are here. I don't see a picture of Brooke." The sound of jostling came through. "Security has already been here, but short of catching someone out of place on a camera, there's not really much they can do," she told me, voice full of sympathy.

And from what Eli had said, the chances of anyone catching Ross or his associate on a camera was slim. But why would they take Brooke's picture?

My eyes met Eli's. "No, that's fine. I can meet with them when I get back."

"Are you sure, dear?"

Meredith still sounded anxious. My heart ached that she'd been drawn into this, however peripherally, but there was simply nothing I could do about it right now. "I'm sure. Thank you so much for calling me. I'll see you on Monday."

I clicked off the call, gesturing toward the security feeds with my phone. "They were at the hospital, searching my locker."

Eli immediately got to work. "Was there anything there for them to find?"

I wish there had been. Then this nightmare could end for both myself and Brooke. "No."

Eli brought up a feed that looked like the parking garage I usually parked in. Was that camera new, or had it been there for a while? Had Remi been watching me at work as well as at home?

Eli cracked his knuckles. "Let's see what we can find out then."

Chapter Fourteen

Remi —

"Why the hell didn't you call me?"

We'd been so fucking late. Late, doing stuff that had zero connection with the most important thing in my life right now, and while I'd been gone...

Fuck!

Eli stopped typing, glanced heavenward like he was praying for strength, then swiveled his chair to face me. "What were you gonna do that I couldn't?"

That wasn't the point. The point was that my woman had needed me. Or I'd needed her—to hold her, keep her from breaking apart, going insane. I hadn't been here, damn it.

And I was taking it out on Eli. Shoving a hand through my hair, I took a lap around the room, desperate to walk off the emotion sending my pulse into heart attack territory.

"Leah did try to call, but you were in the high security area at the time. I told her not to worry about it."

Hacr Technologies, the company my father had founded and passed on to us, his sons, worked with high-tech research that sometimes required heavy security. Hence the new team from JCL we'd just hired on. The tour today had taken us inside parts of the facility where cell phones weren't allowed. I'd thought it would be okay, just a few minutes.

I'd been wrong.

"Fuck."

Saying it aloud gave me much more relief than just thinking it. I walked back to Eli's desk.

"Remi..." He ran a hand over his face. He'd been up almost forty-eight hours straight, working to find intel for us. The dark circles under his eyes shot arrows of guilt at my heart. "There was no threat, just a report. Nothing was stolen. It was a search-and-seize mission, only there was nothing to seize. No direct threat to Leah, okay?"

Not okay, but as Eli was kindly pointing out—instead of calling me a dipshit—there was nothing we could do about it. "Okay." I took the chair next to his. "Did you pull anything from the cameras?"

When I'd first arrived with Leah, I'd given Eli access to the remote cameras I'd placed around the hospital while I'd been "watching" her. The answer was written on my brother's face, no matter how much I didn't want to accept it.

"No more than I found yesterday. Joe Southerland went in. I caught him on a couple of internal cameras, traced him to the area near the locker rooms. When he came back out, freeway, exit, vanish." He twisted his chair back around. "Gimme something to work with, dipshits!"

Better they were the dipshits than me, I guessed.

This was getting us nowhere but exhausted. If Eli couldn't find anything, it wasn't there to find. We were going to have to change focus to tomorrow's meet. Knowing it was time, I made an executive decision.

"Go to bed, bro." I slapped his shoulder. "We'll have any new intel waiting for us in the morning. There's really nothing we can do beyond that."

Eli hung his head; he didn't want to accept that decree any more than I did, but we both knew it was true. Finally, after squaring his shoulders, he gave the mouse a couple of clicks, shoved his chair back, and turned away from the bank of screens. "I'll get a notification if anything suspicious comes up. And"— a hand rose, forestalling the words ready to exit my mouth—"you'll be the first to know if anything does." He barged past me toward the elevator. "Dipshit."

The curse pulled a reluctant laugh out of me as I joined him. The laugh died when the doors slid closed.

I cleared my throat. "Where is she?"

"Upstairs." Eli stared at his shoes. "I'm sorry, Remi; I really am. I'd give anything to have some piece of information that let me tell her, 'Right there, that's where Brooke is.' But I can't."

"Me too." We were warriors, not miracle workers. It didn't matter that Leah got it. We expected more from ourselves.

Eli exited on the first floor, and I continued to the third, needing to get this monkey suit off and into something I could relax in. Despite being homeless most of our childhood and Levi being the only boss I'd ever known, I enjoyed the structure and discipline at Hacr. The scientists there made field-changing discoveries; the security facilitated those changes. If I'd been someone else, if my parents hadn't been murdered...

I walked down the hall, shrugging out of the jacket on the way. What I didn't like about Hacr was the formality it required, at least for us. The Agozi family had an image to uphold, and that meant suits. Why I couldn't just wear my fatigues like every other member of the security team, I didn't know. And weapons. Even the thick layers of my formal clothing couldn't make up for the fact that I was naked without my weapons. But no one at Hacr knew our background, knew we were as capable as their security officers—more, probably—to deal with threats.

Here at home? When I left my room in sweats and a T-shirt, I had more than one weapon on me.

My knock on Leah's door got no answer. Pushing inside, I was met with a dark, silent room. No light filtered beneath the bathroom door, so no Leah there, probably. Only when my eyes adjusted enough could I see the slight mound beneath the cream-colored sheets on the bed. She didn't stir as I approached.

"Leah?"

No response, only the slow rise and fall of her chest telling me exhaustion had gotten the better of her. I set my gun on the nightstand, climbed under the covers, and did what I'd hungered to do since I'd walked into the bat cave and heard about the call—I snuggled up behind her.

A ragged sigh escaped Leah when my arm settled across her belly, but she didn't wake, not then and not when I pulled her into the curve of my body. The silence wrapped around us like a warm blanket, turning tense muscles liquid and soothing the runaway thoughts in my head. Warriors knew to sleep when given the slightest opportunity. I knew to be grateful for the slightest bit of peace, and I reveled in it now.

At least until Leah stirred in my arms. Seconds later her body went rigid.

"It's all right, just me," I murmured into her hair. "Remi."

My name, husky in her sleep-roughened voice. Blood surged to my cock without my permission. "Yeah."

Leah tried to turn, to face me, but I tightened my arms. *Just a few minutes longer.* Or a lifetime. I wasn't anywhere near ready to let go.

She stilled. Relaxed. Her body went boneless against mine in an age-old display of trust. Leah wasn't submissive, not anywhere else, but here, now, she was surrendering her body to my demands. It was the kind of gift a man like me would never dream of receiving because we didn't deserve it.

Leah gave it anyway, hardening my cock even more.

"They were searching my locker at work," she finally said.

The traces of fear beneath the words made my fists tighten. I deliberately opened them, smoothed them over her skin in slow circles. "I know. Eli filled me in."

"They're going to keep looking"—the rise and fall of her chest got faster—"and they're not gonna find anything. And tomorrow when we meet them, we won't have what they're demanding of us." Leah's breath hitched. "How am I going to keep her safe?"

I jostled her against me. "You don't have to. We will."

"I'm actually starting to believe that."

I couldn't stop myself—I threw a leg over hers, tucking her even closer. My cock rode the ridge of her spine, but she didn't pull away.

"I'm starting to trust you with a lot of things, Jeremiah." Leah's words whispered between us in the dark, the sound of my name on her lips sending more heat to my groin. "Maybe I shouldn't, but I am."

"Is it so bad to trust me?" *To love me?*

My heart thumped in my throat as I waited for her reply.

"After Angelo..." She turned her head to stare up at the ceiling. "I never wanted to risk feeling anything for another man ever again. Brooke was all I needed." She shrugged, dropped her head back to the pillow, hiding her face from me. "And then I met you."

Maybe it was better that I couldn't read her. That she couldn't read me. As much as I'd craved this moment, wanted her to be the air I breathed, I had to warn her. "I'm not a good man, Leah."

She scooted onto her back, then faced me. "That's what I thought too. But you're more good than either of us could see. You care about an innocent child being kidnapped. You care about me being safe." Her hand appeared out of the darkness to trace the stubble roughening my cheeks. "I can see it; I know it's there. But I'm afraid to trust it."

She shouldn't. I believed that, but I wasn't going to remind her of it. Instead I turned until my lips brushed the center of her palm. "Why?"

Her eyes glittered in the dim light. "I trusted Angelo. I trusted Ross." She shrugged. "I'm afraid that this, that all the good I'm seeing, will end up being another lie in the end."

I was who I was. Everything I'd given her had been the truth, but she wouldn't believe my words if I told her. Only actions.

"And when I touched you?" I brought my hand up this time, tilting her chin until she had no choice but to meet my eyes. "Was that a lie?"

A tear escaped Leah's eye. "That might be the most truthful thing I've ever felt." She leaned her body away. "But I shouldn't be feeling this, not with Brooke—"

I tugged her back to me. "There's no 'shouldn't' here, Leah. Nothing wrong with surviving the night with me."

"Is that what we're doing?"

No. I'm loving you.

"Yes." I took her mouth then, to stop me from saying something she couldn't accept. To stop myself from spilling my soul. Tomorrow my brothers and I would be ready to find Brooke and bring her home. I'd do that for Leah, even if it led straight to letting go of them both.

But not tonight. Tonight was mine.

Chapter Fifteen

Remi —

Her mouth was salty from earlier tears, from crying when I hadn't been here to hold her. She deserved so much more than crying alone in the dark. I was a poor substitute for the man she did deserve, but I'd take what the universe would give me.

Leah opened to me, let my tongue inside. Moaned around it. This woman that I'd dreamed about for so long was finally in my arms. I dug my fingers into her hair and tilted until the angle was just right for me to get deeper, to overpower her with the hunger pounding through my veins. With the need for moist walls gripping more than just my tongue.

Leah shifted from her back to her side to press closer. With my leg over her, my cock was forced right against the join of her thighs. Right where I wanted it to be. I rocked instinctively, my cock head hitting her clit every time—tap, tap, tap. She whimpered, squirmed against me, gripped my shirt with both fists and pulled to get me closer. To get off on nothing more than the press of my dick.

No way in hell.

I tore myself away. "Clothes. Off."

I didn't know if the command was for me or her. I didn't care. I only knew I needed to be skin to skin with her, needed to feel her body beneath my hands, wrapping tight around my cock. In seconds my shirt and sweats were on the floor; then I went to work on Leah's.

Grasping the hem of her shirt, I yanked it over her head. When her fingers went to the front clasp of her bra, I jerked them away. "Mine." It was all I could get out. Forget fucking sentences—one-word demands seemed to be all I was capable of. Thank fuck my body would move without actual thought. I twisted the clasp between two fingers and peeled back the cups to reveal the prettiest breasts I'd ever seen. Plump, round, with thick nipples that already reached for me, telling me what she hungered for. Abandoning the bra, I leaned over and sucked one tight tip into my mouth.

"Remi!"

Holy shit. She tasted so good, like midnight with a hint of salt and the sweetest cream. I sucked over and over, frantic for more, for her to feed me everything she had. Grasping her around the ribs, I rolled us until Leah straddled my stomach, her breasts right in my face, all I could see—all I wanted to see. Nothing mattered but this.

I scraped my teeth along her nipple, then moved to the other side. Leah was chanting my name, rolling her hips to get the friction she needed against my stomach. Her breasts were sensitive, I discovered, sending her right to the edge just as fast as feasting on them had me. They filled my hands as I cupped them, holding them close, moving from one to the other with lips and teeth and tongue attacking until Leah gave a frantic cry and orgasmed above me.

I couldn't tear my eyes away. So. Fucking. Beautiful.

She was still gasping for air when I rolled her to my side. "What—"

"I need to see you, all of you, Leah." Every last inch. Her bra went first, then the jeans she'd fallen asleep in. Her panties were lace, surprising me. She was so practical, so fierce, that seeing the delicate fabric made me pause. Here was the tender heart of my warrior, the soft, vulnerable underbelly. I leaned down to kiss the faint marks along her belly from where she'd carried Brooke—the marks of a fighter— as I drew off the thin panties and exposed her fully to me for the first time.

The scent of her arousal filled my nose. "Fuck." I moved lower, sucking in gulps of that scent, savoring the sign of her need. *For me.* "Fuck, Leah. You smell so fucking good."

She squirmed. I didn't know if it was need or embarrassment; it didn't matter. Either way, I was getting between those legs. Leah didn't protest as I crawled over her, as I made a place for myself in the vee of her body. My shoulders pushed at her inner thighs until they were split wide, allowing me in, exposing the most intimate parts of her body to my intent gaze.

This was Leah. *My* Leah. My warrior.

I licked straight up her center, opening her shyly closed lips to me. Leah screamed, the sound muffled like she was covering her mouth, holding herself back. Hiding her need from me.

I couldn't allow her to hide.

Grabbing both hands, I forced them down to her sides. A tug on her wrists pulled her even closer to me. "Let go, Leah. This is for you. Tonight is for you." I dug my nose into the neatly trimmed curls atop her mound, rubbed her scent onto my skin like the animal I felt myself becoming. "No one can hear you. Let go."

And then I feasted.

Cries filled my ears as I devoured every inch of her pussy. Labia, clit, the shadowed entrance to her body. I licked and sucked and tugged with my teeth. I blew warm air against her, watching her shiver, then speared her with my tongue and felt her walls contract around me. And all the while I stared up her body, past those perfect breasts to the unguarded face that showed me what she needed, what she hungered for. Leah, completely open. Completely mine.

I pushed deep, my nose nudging her clit. Cream coated my tongue as the pleasure took her over the edge.

I had to feel it. Pushing to my knees, I lined my cock up and thrust inside, straight to the hilt. I needed those contractions, needed to immerse myself in the pleasure I'd given her, feel her walls wrapping so tight around me as she lost herself.

Leah jerked against me. "Remi!"

My hands wrapped almost completely around her hips, big enough to hold her in place. "Relax." The word came out more croak than anything, the need to thrust hammering at me. I wouldn't give in, not yet. I needed this. "Just give it a minute."

A strained chuckle left her lips. "Easier said than done when you've got a log shoved inside you."

"This log waited as long as it could," I told her, the words gravel-rough. "You feel so good, Leah. All tight and wet and..." A groan escaped me. I had to stop talking before I lost it completely. "Just breathe. For both of us."

Her hands came up to rest on her lower belly, pressing lightly. Feeling me inside her. "So full," she moaned.

My cock jerked hard, threatening to spill. I loved that she wasn't inhibited, that everything she felt was right out there for me to see. I couldn't get enough of staring down at her body, all that creamy skin, the hills and valleys, the open honesty of her beautiful eyes.

"Leah...God. You—"

I clamped my lips shut before things escaped that I couldn't take back. Things like love and want and forever. Things I could never have, no matter how much they pounded in my brain, begging to be let out.

Leah circled her hips, and a new flood of arousal bathed my cock. "Remi, I need... I need it. Please."

I eased back, continuing to hold her still. Glancing down, I could see the wetness on my body, see it dripping from hers. See the invasion as I pushed back inside.

We groaned together.

I pulled back again, breathing away the need to blow, to spurt inside her and bathe her with my come. I focused on my cock, on her lips clinging to me, begging me to stay, to come back, to—

And that's when I realized.

"Fuck." I pulled all the way out. "Fuck, fuck, fuck."

Leah came up on her elbow, a confused frown on her face. "What is it?"

"Condom," I muttered, reaching for the bedside table.

Her eyes clamped closed, and a curse of her own escaped her.

"I've got it," I said, ripping open a packet and sliding the latex over my cock. My angry cock. Nothing should come between us, even the thinnest barrier. I needed to feel her, to have her feel me. But I also needed to protect her, always.

Fuck.

I slid back inside, glanced up to see Leah's eyes glittering at me in the dark. "Okay?"

She didn't say anything for a moment, didn't move. Then, "Putting it on now doesn't mean we didn't do something incredibly stupid."

I planted my fists on either side of her ribs, leaning over her. Leah's eyes went a little dazed at the pressure against her clit. "I know. I'm sorry."

She tilted her pelvis, taking me deeper. "It's on both of us, Remi, not just you."

She was wrong about that, but I wasn't going to argue with my cock screaming at me to move and Leah's willing body lying beneath mine. Instead I came down over her, nuzzled the valley between her breasts. A small bite of one sweet curve drew a gasp from her lips. "Ready?"

Her knees tightened around me. "Holy hell, yes."

A tight feeling hit my chest, took my breath. Trailing my tongue along the skin I'd just nipped, I spread my knees and slid a hand under Leah's hips. The lift put her at just the right height for me to drive in all the way to the hilt. "Holy hell is right," I whispered against her skin. Grasping her nipple between my teeth, I sucked hard. She arched into me as I rolled my hips back, then slammed inside.

Leah cried out. Groaned. Begged. Clawed my back, my ass, and demanded more, harder, faster. I gave her everything she needed, everything I had. It took way too long and not nearly long enough, but in the end we hit the peak together, shattering into what felt like a million pieces, scattered together on the sweaty silken sheets.

Arms tight around Leah's body like I thought she'd disappear into thin air, I held her against me and struggled to breathe, to think. To pull myself back together. And when I had, I tilted her face up for my kiss and started all over again.

Chapter Sixteen

Leah —

Remi barely let me sleep. Maybe that's why, when he stirred, I did too. And groaned. I felt like I'd been carved out and left empty. Hit by a six-four, 260-pound storm that had battered me, body and soul. God knew I'd be walking funny when I finally got out of this bed.

Remi stretched behind me, then curled around my back. "You okay?"

I was never going to be okay again; I'd known that from the very first kiss. "Sure."

"Liar." His palm flattened on my lower stomach, pulling another groan from me. "Don't lie to me, Leah. Not after last night." The words sounded disappointed, like he'd expected more. But he didn't wait around for me to answer. Moving toward his side of the bed, he said, "I'll run a bath for you."

I wanted to tell him not to bother, wanted to deny how he'd affected me—emotionally and physically—but I couldn't. He was right; he'd given me too much of himself last night. The least I could do was give him the truth. "Thank you, Remi."

"Sure."

A long soak in the tub did help ease the sore muscles. It also gave me time to inventory the marks on my body: love bites on my breasts, red swollen nipples, finger marks on my hips, my inner thighs. I'd have to check my neck when I got out. As much as Eli's teasing nature helped lighten the mood sometimes, I felt too raw, too vulnerable for anyone to know about this. I needed time.

The one thing I didn't really have today. Because we were going after Brooke in a few short hours. Remi had promised.

By the time I made it to the kitchen, breakfast was well underway. Stealing myself, I walked up to the stove where Remi was flipping pancakes. "Hey."

He paused, his gaze taking me in from the raised collar of my plaid button-down—there had definitely been a hickey—to my sweaty palms rubbing up and down my jean-clad thighs. "Hey." He finished flipping the rest of the pancakes, laid down the spatula, and then I was in his arms.

"Good morning, *lev sheli*." He breathed the words against the sensitive skin just below my ear.

I swallowed hard against the lump in my throat. How did he do this? How did a man I was pretty sure wouldn't hesitate to kill make me melt with his tenderness? Last night he'd overwhelmed me, but in the midst of the storm there had been moments like this. Moments where I knew he cared, that I wasn't just a convenient screw. Moments that planted dreams of a happily ever after that simply wasn't meant to be.

"What does *lev sheli*"—the words didn't roll near as smoothly off my tongue—"mean?"

He nipped my earlobe. "Something my father called my mother." Sadness flashed in his gaze before he forced a smile. "I'll explain it sometime."

Something his dad had called his mom? More melting, damn it.

"Pancakes are burning," Eli pointed out behind Remi's back.

"Then do something about it, dickhead." But Remi let me go, his fingers sliding reluctantly from my hips. I turned toward the coffeepot, only to be pinned by three pairs of wide, curious eyes.

So much for no one knowing what had happened last night. I tugged my collar tighter around my throat and hurried to get myself some caffeine.

When we were all seated at the table, plates stacked with light, fluffy pancakes and crispy bacon, Levi speared me with those inscrutable gray eyes. "You have the phone."

I fished my cell from my pocket and laid it beside my plate on the table. Such a small bit of plastic and electricity to be the only lifeline to my baby.

"They'll call soon," Remi said. "Likely they won't give us much warning, try and keep us off-kilter, unable to prepare."

"How will we prepare?" I asked.

"Not *we*," Remi growled. "You're staying here."

"Like hell I am."

"Leah—"

"She's right," Levi interrupted. "Think with your instincts and not your dick. As much as you want to protect her, she has to be there. Ross will insist on it."

I winced at the dick comment but let it pass for now. "Brooke will need me there," I pointed out. "She doesn't know any of you. She won't feel safe, and she might try to fight you. You need her calm and cooperative." And I needed to be the one to do that for her. As soon as possible, not hours after Remi managed to extract her. "I can take care of Brooke.

That leaves you all to take care of the rest without worrying about her."

The skin around Remi's eyes went tight, broadcasting his worry, but he gave me a nod anyway. "You do exactly what we tell you, Leah, got it?"

"Of course." These men had been together all their lives, knew each other inside and out. I was an anomaly in their well-oiled machine. "I trust you."

Remi's eyes rounded. I hadn't realized what I was going to say before the words escaped. Hadn't even realized it was true, but…it was. "I trust you," I said again.

The flare of heat and something soft, tender in his eyes shook me right down to my toes.

Love, Leah. That's love.

It wasn't. Couldn't be. But it still made me melt.

Levi cleared his throat. "Remi will go in with you. Eli and I will take the outside."

I forced my gaze away from Remi's. "What will happen to Ross after…" I set my fork down, no longer hungry. "Afterward?"

Remi reached for me, tugged at my chin until I met his eyes again. "That's up to you, Leah."

A lump of fear caught in my throat. "Killing him isn't going to get the Fiori family to leave us alone."

"No, it's not." The warm amber of his eyes iced over. "If you were anyone else, we wouldn't be having this discussion; Ross would be a dead man walking for what he's done to you, to Brooke. But he's your brother, so I'll give you the choice. We can give them a chance to surrender to authorities if that's what you want."

"And you won't hurt him?"

Remi's mouth tightened into a grim line. "Not much."

I knew from his face that was the best I was going to get. And maybe, deep down inside, brother or not, I thought Ross deserved whatever punishment Remi chose to dish out. "Just don't kill him."

Remi nodded. I turned to Levi. "I still don't know what to do about the Fioris. I don't have what they want," I said for what felt like the thousandth time.

"We'll worry about that after Brooke is back with her mother."

I shook my head. "Why? Why are you all doing this, risking this for me?"

Levi took his empty plate and stood, staring at Remi for a long moment before turning away. "You're a part of us now."

Because I had slept with his brother? Or because Remi had brought me here? I wasn't sure which answer I wanted, so I clamped my mouth shut on any further questions.

Abby was smiling at her plate. Eli popped the last bite of pancake into his mouth, mumbling around it, "Does that mean she gets dish duty? Because I'm starting to get dishpan hands, yo."

Remi smacked the back of Eli's head. "Keep talking and you also get to clean every weapon in the weapons locker."

Eli shot his brother an evil look but began gathering dishes anyway.

I grinned.

My cell rang.

The room went instantly still, silent. Another ring.

"Remi," I whimpered. I'd thought, coming to this point, I'd be eager, confident. But I wasn't. One wrong move could get my daughter killed.

"You've got this, *lev sheli.*"

The men in the room stirred as if surprised.

I reached for the phone. "What does it mean?" I asked without looking at him.

"It means…" He shook his head, sighed. "You're *eshet hayil*, Leah. My warrior woman. Answer the phone."

Warrior woman. I didn't feel like a warrior at the moment, but I could pretend.

The phone rang in my hand. I clicked the Answer button, then Speaker. "Ross?"

"Leah, it's me."

His voice sounded higher than normal. Excited. No, scared.

What was Ross afraid of?

"We've got the location. Write it down."

I glanced at Remi, saw him keying the address into his phone. He gave me a sharp nod.

"Got it, Ross." I took a deep breath. "Let me speak to Brooke."

I could hear Ross moving around but couldn't make out any distinctive sounds. "Not now. This afternoon. Meet us at one; you'll see her then."

"Is she all right?" I had to know. Four hours from now was too long to wait. "Is she?"

Ross hesitated, making my heart jump. "She's fine," he finally said. "I promise, Leah." More movement. "This afternoon, come alone, got it? And bring the recordings."

Those damn recordings. In that moment, if Angelo had still been alive, I thought I might kill him myself. All this, the danger to our daughter, for nothing.

"Not going to happen, Windon, and you know it," Remi said.

I opened my mouth to protest. Remi held up a finger, his eyes seeming to say it would be all right.

"She comes alone or no deal," Ross said. This time the quiver was definitely fear. Of Remi or someone else?

"I come with her or I bring a team in and destroy your ass. Which will it be?"

My lungs ached, making me realize I was holding my breath.

Curses filtered through the phone. "Fine, then. But you only. No one else."

The call clicked off. I dropped the phone onto the table like a hot potato.

"And if he believes that, I have some rice fields in China that would make nice building sites," Eli said. The words were joking, but his tone... I'd never seen it in him before, the killer instinct, but now I understood. It might be buried beneath a lighthearted facade, but it was there nonetheless.

Abby took the dishes from Eli's hands. "I'll take care of cleanup. Y'all have planning to do."

Remi picked up the phone, handed it to me. I slid it into my pocket. "Let's go," he said, holding out his hand.

I took it. "Let's go."

It was time to get my daughter back.

Chapter Seventeen

Leah —

I eyed the aerial image of the address Ross had given us on the table nearby. "We're going in the front, right?"

Remi tightened the strap under my arm. The Kevlar vest was sized for one of the brothers, not a smaller woman, so no amount of tightening would make it fit, but something was better than nothing, Remi had said. In this case I agreed.

"Right."

"And your brothers are already in place?"

Remi began strapping on his own vest. "Outside the warehouse, yeah." He slapped the Velcro hard. "We're not certain it's only Windon and Southerland at the meet, so better to be safe than sorry. My brothers will take care of any outside guards before coming in to assist."

Through the rear of the building, effectively flanking the enemy. We'd gone over the plan more than once, but I found myself obsessing over every detail, worrying I'd forget something, get it wrong, even though I knew the fear was ludicrous. There weren't that many steps, for goodness' sake.

That was the problem. My daughter's life depended on each and every one.

Remi put on a blue button-down over his vest and tucked it into his pants. I couldn't help noticing the vest made him look bigger, more intimidating. Definitely sexy. "This is going to work, Leah."

"You and your brothers have done this before?" I asked absently.

"Not this, exactly." He slid a handgun into a holster on his calf. "Usually we don't have to worry about anyone surviving but us."

My heart jumped into my throat. "What?"

One side of Remi's mouth tugged up. "Hey, we kept ourselves alive so far." The smile slid away as he cupped my cheek, his thumb stroking my skin. "We know what we're doing, Leah."

Digging his fingers into my hair to hold me in place, he gave me one of those quick, hard kisses like he'd given me before he left with King. When he drew back, I could literally see the shift—in his body, his eyes. All emotion slid away, leaving behind a stone-cold killer I'd never seen before. "I'll take care of her. And you. I promise."

Without another word, he turned for the door.

Abby stepped close to hug me. "He really will," she said in my ear. For the briefest moment I let her warmth surround me, ground me. "They won't fail. In a couple of hours you'll have Brooke back with you, safe and sound."

I couldn't accept anything less. And part of that was up to me, so I straightened, breathing through the fear to a kind of calm resolve I'd never felt before. Was this how Remi felt, how he turned off the emotion to focus on the job at hand? Not because he wanted to, but because he had to in order to bring everyone home safe. Hurrying after him out the door, I prayed I could be just as strong as he was.

That's what Brooke needed. I could fall apart later.

The drive into town was silent. Only when I knew we were a few minutes out did I break from my thoughts enough to speak.

"Remi, I need… I want to ask you something. A favor." Sort of.

"What?"

His tone was clipped, but I didn't take it personally. He was in warrior mode. Exactly where I needed him to be. "If anything happens—"

"It won't."

I squeezed my eyes closed, took a deep breath. When I opened them, it was to the reality of a mostly abandoned industrial park on the edge of town. *Almost there.* "If it does, I want your promise that Brooke's welfare comes first. You keep her safe, no matter what. She's a little girl. If you have to make a choice—her or me—you go to her."

I looked at him then, needing to see the promise in his expression, not just hear the words. Remi's mouth was tight, his eyes narrowed—unhappy. He didn't want to give me that promise.

That moment, between one breath and the next, was when the truth finally settled in my heart. I had sensed all along that this thing between us wasn't just an obsession, a weird attraction. I'd known love before, with Angelo. I'd felt it, seen it. Remi would never hesitate to put a child's life above all else unless the person he'd have to abandon meant everything to him.

Unless I meant everything to him.

"Please," I begged. "Promise me."

He blew out a breath. "I'll do whatever I have to do to get you both out safe."

"Remi—"

"Stop." His fists tightened on the steering wheel before deliberately relaxing. "It's the most I can give you, Leah. *Both of you* will come out of this alive. I won't accept anything less."

I subsided as the warehouse came into view at the end of a deserted road. Remi parked the SUV several yards away. We'd walk from here, allowing Ross's friend to see that we were alone.

It took one glance to realize Ross and Southerland definitely weren't.

"Remi?"

His face was grim as he stared at the vehicles parked on either side of the building, the guards patrolling outside. "We planned for this. It'll be fine."

I didn't see how it could be fine, not when two targets had become at least six, and that was only outside. But I had to trust that Remi knew what he was talking about; there was no other choice. "Okay."

We got out.

The men at the front of the warehouse came to attention, their guns aiming our way as we walked toward them. I scanned the trees nearby, the empty buildings we passed, but caught no sign of Remi's brothers. Oddly enough, that knowledge sent calm rushing over me. Secure in the Agozi brothers' expertise, I walked forward with my head held high and no more than the slightest tremor at facing down six gun barrels.

"Gentlemen," Remi said when we were in earshot, "you're expecting us."

One man, as big as Remi and looking just as tough, motioned us forward. "Inside."

We were stopped at the door and patted down. The big guy took Remi, smirking as he pulled the gun from his ankle holster. The man frisking me took extra pleasure in feeling me up under my vest. I barely held back the need to break his nose with my elbow, reminding myself that these men would get what was coming to them in just a few minutes.

We were finally allowed to proceed.

Inside the warehouse we found a big, empty, gloomy room—or mostly empty. In the center sat Brooke, tied to a chair. Ross stood beside her, his hand on her shoulder, Southerland on the opposite side. And half a dozen armed men behind them.

"Mommy!"

My heart kicked at Brooke's cry, the way she struggled against the ropes. Ross bent to her ear, saying something that had very little effect on my daughter. Needing her calm, afraid of what Southerland would do if she caused trouble, I hurried forward. "It's all right, baby. I'm here. It's okay."

"That's close enough," Southerland said when I was a few yards out. His gun hand came up, the muzzle pointing at Brooke's head.

I jerked to a stop. "Please. Please don't do that." I brought my hands out, showing them empty. "I won't come any closer." Brooke's terrified eyes yanked at me, urging me to help her, but I forced myself to stay still. "It's okay, baby. I promise."

God, if something happened and her last moments on this earth were filled with fear—

No! No. I wouldn't think that way. We were getting her out. Nothing else was acceptable.

"I didn't know they'd be here, Leah," Ross said. "It was supposed to be you and me, that's all."

Southerland lifted his gun without looking away from me and pulled the trigger. Brooke's scream mingled with mine.

Ross dropped to his knees, leaning heavily against Brooke's chair, a hand clutching his side. Red washed through his fingers. "Leah—" he wheezed.

"He's no longer of use to me," Southerland said, lowering his gun to Brooke's head again. "If she's not either, you know what happens next."

"No! Don't hurt her." I took a step forward.

Remi grabbed my arm, stopping me. "We told Ross and we'll tell you," he said. "Leah doesn't have the recordings. She never did. The fact that your men were too incompetent to find them in Angelo's things is your problem, not ours."

Southerland cocked his head, his stare boring into Remi. "I've heard of you. You took out Jonathan Axe's team a while back."

"The whole team," Remi said. I could hear the satisfaction filling his voice, and shivered. "But you got one thing wrong."

Southerland smirked. "What's that?"

"I didn't take out Axe's team. My brother did." Remi grinned, the sight sadistic in its amusement. "One man, one team. But there are three of us now."

The men behind Southerland shifted uneasily, more than one glancing up at the few windows giving meager light to the room.

Not Southerland. "Three what?"

"Three brothers, motherfucker," Remi said. And grinned. Outside, the distinct sound of gunshots filled the air. Six shots, so loud I ducked.

Southerland swung toward the nearest window, eyes going wide. Remi charged.

"Brooke!"

I was halfway across the room when she slipped from her chair, Ross still pulling at the ropes. "Mommy!"

Trusting Remi to deal with Southerland, I rushed forward. Shouts came from the back of the room. Shots echoed, deafeningly loud in the empty space. I ignored it all to complete the one mission I had come here for: to get my daughter. Scooping her tiny body up in my arms, I turned to run for the door, terror racing through me with every step, every heartbeat.

But Remi had promised, and he delivered. I burst through the door into the sunlight, my baby clutched in my arms. Brooke was sobbing, her fingers digging into my neck, her arms practically strangling me. I didn't stop. *Get to the truck. Get to the truck.* Only when I had Brooke safely inside the SUV with the doors locked did I even breathe.

And that's when I lost it.

I have no idea how long we sat there, Brooke and me, hugging and crying and rocking. How many times I whispered "I love you" and "Mommy is here" and "you're safe now." I only knew that when knuckles rapped on the window near my head, I actually screamed.

Eli stood outside, his stare intent as he waited for me to open the door.

I pushed at the latch. "Yes?"

He gripped the door, swinging it wide. "You need to come back inside," he said. "I can keep her for you."

"No, Eli, she stays with me."

He shook his head. "You don't want her to see what's in there, Leah. Trust me." He glanced from Brooke, still clutching my neck, her head turned away as if she couldn't bear to look at anyone right now. "It's Ross. You need to come."

Ross had been shot. I squeezed Brooke closer. "I am— Okay."

But Brooke was having none of her letting me go.

"Can you cover…whatever she'd see?" I asked.

"We can't. Too much evidence left behind," he explained. Over a dozen bodies? Yeah, I bet that was too much evidence already. I doubted the guys carried sheets or whatever to cover dead bodies. And carting them all out of here would be impossible.

I couldn't believe I was thinking through the problem of hiding dead bodies.

"We've taken care of anything pointing to Brooke's presence, but, Leah"—he glanced over his shoulder again—"you need to hurry."

I thought about the shot Ross had taken, the angle, the blood— My heart clenched tight. "Right."

Sliding out of the SUV, I whispered in Brooke's ear, "You're with me, babe, okay? Just keep your eyes closed. Mommy's got you." As we walked I said to Eli, "Give me your shirt."

Like Remi, he wore a button-down over his vest. He stripped it off, and before walking through the door, I threw the shirt over Brooke's head, murmuring reassurances to her the entire time.

The warehouse was a bloodbath. I tried hard to ignore that as I rushed across to where Remi knelt beside Ross, now laid out on the floor. "Leah." Ross reached for me as I slid to my knees, taking Remi's place. Eyes hazy with pain and something I prayed was regret, he reached for Brooke's leg where it rested at my hip. "I'm sorry."

You should be. The words were right there on the tip of my tongue, but I held them back. Ross had done something I'd probably never forgive him for, but he wouldn't be around to live with that knowledge. I couldn't bear to have him die with it. "I know."

Ross coughed, spattering blood across his face. "They won't stop," he croaked. "Never."

"I know," I said again.

He reached for my hand, and I grabbed his, gripped it tight. "I took care…" he said. "Didn't hurt her. Promise."

He had. He'd hurt Brooke and me. Tears welled in my eyes. Angry tears. Devastated tears. "Ross—"

"I am…so sorry…Leah." His head tilted back, and a groan escaped his lips. "So…sorry."

I watched as he took a final breath, as his grip went slack in mine. I watched and I cried. For what had been. For what would never be.

And then I stood up and took my daughter out of there.

Chapter Eighteen

Remi —

We were fast, and we were fucking lethal. But as much as I had wanted to wipe every last man in this place off the face of the earth, Leah's brother had not been marked for death.

He was dead anyway.

I'd seen the look in Leah's eyes, the blank look survivors have when everything has just been too much and you can't really register any more. She'd clung to Brooke as hard as Brooke was clinging to her, the only sure thing in a tsunami of events she couldn't control. It would hit her later, but for now her focus was on the only thing that mattered: her daughter.

I shouldn't wish I was included, that I was the one holding them both in my arms, keeping the outside world at bay. This wasn't about me, for fuck's sake.

I stood from where I knelt beside Ross's cooling body. I'd retrieved his phone, making sure nothing else on him or in his pockets pointed to Brooke or her kidnapping. The police would eventually figure out who he and his dead associates were, though probably not why they were all here, in this abandoned warehouse, with bullets in their bodies. The people who were important knew, and that was all that mattered. For now at least.

The back door to the warehouse banged open, and Eli stepped through, dragging the last body in from outside. Levi followed with a five-gallon container of gasoline. Cleanup duty. I walked toward them.

"Leah's in the SUV," Eli said, his voice strained as he pulled two hundred pounds of deadweight to the middle of the room.

I stripped off my gloves and added them to the center pile. "I'm taking them home."

"Home?" Levi set the container on the concrete. Straightening, he pierced me with a look. "Do we need to talk about this, brother?"

About my woman? About what would happen next? "No." I turned away. "Nothing to talk about." We all knew this was temporary. Even after what I'd said to Leah this morning, even after calling her *lev sheli*—a name that told my brothers everything they needed to know about my feelings for her—this had never been anything more than a temporary situation. Leah had her daughter back. She'd watched us cold-bloodedly kill a dozen men. There was no room for a morally questionable assassin in that family unit.

Levi let me go. Outside, I hurried toward the SUV, frustration boiling inside at my inability to see through the darkly tinted glass to the woman I loved. Though it had been no more than twenty minutes since she had walked out of the warehouse, when I opened the driver's side door, it was to the sight of Leah dozing in the front seat. Adrenaline drop. Brooke lay in her lap, her little girl features grubby from fear and crying, sound asleep.

Leah stirred when I closed my door.

"It's all right," I told her, reaching to turn the key in the ignition. "Go back to sleep. I'll wake you when we get back to the house."

She reached for the seat belt and pulled it across her and Brooke's bodies. "She won't let me go," she said quietly. "She should be in the back, in her own belt—really in her booster seat—but when I tried to put her back there, she refused to let me go."

I took the belt from her and buckled it securely. "I'll get you both back safe; don't worry."

Leah stroked Brooke's hair back from her forehead, worry lining her face. I'd seen Brooke hundreds of times, but I don't think I'd realized just how closely she resembled Leah until now, seeing them side by side. The same hair, the same arch to their eyebrows, the same full mouth. What part of Angelo had lived on in his daughter?

"I don't think she's really slept this whole time," Leah said, her voice wobbling.

Likely not. I remembered what that was like. When my brothers and I had been on the street, we always had to be alert to the faintest hint of trouble, always aware that any security you thought you had, could and did disappear in an instant. The difference between my brothers and Brooke was that she'd gotten her security back. She'd sleep like the dead for a while now that she was in her mother's arms.

I turned the SUV around and headed out.

"What about..." Leah reached up to rub at her eyes. "What about all that back there?"

What we had left behind. "We took care of it." She didn't need to know how.

"And...Ross?"

She might find our solution hard to deal with, but Ross was beyond caring. "He'll be with the others. They'll find him…eventually."

Leah took a shaky breath, then let it out. "I should contact my father."

The man who didn't know she was alive. He would gain one child back while losing the other. "Not yet. We need time to plan before any of this gets out."

"Okay."

It wasn't a Leah answer, but it was one she'd given me too often today. She sounded tired. Not just tired—weary down to her bones. It made my heart ache in a way I'd never experienced before.

It also made me wish I could kill Southerland with my bare hands all over again.

I parked in the front drive almost an hour later. "Wait there," I told Leah as she stirred. "I'll come around and help you out."

Brooke was still asleep. I opened Leah's door, took her arm to steady her as she stepped onto the running board, then down to the drive. "Need me to take her?" I asked. I knew exactly zero about caring for children, but Brooke wasn't a baby; I knew she would be heavy to carry all the way up the stairs.

Leah paused, and her eyes met mine. "No"—she cleared her throat—"but thank you, Remi." She walked toward the door. "For everything."

It sounded too much like goodbye. I trailed Leah as she walked inside, past Abby holding the door, to the elevator. When she stepped in, I stayed back, uncertain for what might be the first time in my life. "Tell me if you need anything."

Leah gave me a vague smile as the doors closed, already a million miles away.

That ache in my heart got stronger.

Unsure what to do with myself—and hating that uncertainty—I wandered into the kitchen. Abby was standing at the stove, the rich scent of tomato soup rising from the pot she stirred. She glanced up as I settled on a stool at the center island. "She took Brooke upstairs?"

I nodded. Should I go up there? Stay here and let Leah and Brooke have their time together? Would she turn me away if I showed up? She didn't need now that Brooke was safe, did she?

Doubt clawed at me, which just pissed me the hell off. I wasn't this guy. I didn't hesitate. Hell, I'd decided to steal Leah from her home in seconds. My life or death had often depended on making split-second decisions under tense conditions. But now?

"Why aren't you up there with her?" Abby asked.

I glared at my brother's lover. "Because..." An ache shot through my fisted hands. "Why would she want me with her?" My usefulness was at an end, just like Ross's. He'd bled out on the cold concrete floor; right now my bleeding out was too damn metaphorical for my taste.

"Remi—"

I shook my head. "It's over, Abby."

Her snort jerked my gaze up to hers.

"And men say we're the dramatic half of the species." Turning the soup down to simmer, she moved to the fridge and began gathering the ingredients for grilled cheese sandwiches. "Remi, no one could see the two of you together and think this was over. Even if you were separated, it wouldn't be over. Besides, this thing with the Fioris—"

"I got her brother killed."

Abby paused in spreading butter over a slice of bread, using her knife to point my way. I almost smiled.

"If Ross is dead, it's his own damn fault. Not yours and certainly not Leah's or Brooke's." She went back to spreading. "And if he's dead, she needs you right now more than ever. Don't stop reaching for her, Remi. Don't give up."

Giving up had never been in my nature; hell, I'd stalked the woman for almost two years. But there'd been something in Leah's voice… "Maybe she wants me to let her go," I said, the words somewhere between a statement and a question.

Abby turned on the burner beneath a pan and set the first sandwich inside. "I see the way she looks at you. That's not the look of a woman who could walk away and never look back."

"She's got a child to think about." I watched Abby press the sandwich with a spatula, urging the cheese to melt. "No woman wants a killer near her child."

Abby turned on me. "I do," she said fiercely. "And I certainly don't see you as a killer."

I closed my eyes, feeling that tight band around my chest loosen the slightest bit. *God, Abby. What did we do to deserve you?* I smiled her way. "We've already established that you're delusional. You chose Levi, after all."

"And I'd do it again in a heartbeat," she said softly, honesty shining from those hazel eyes, making my heart ache all over again. What would that be like, for a woman to choose you, just as you were? Could Leah ever choose me?

"Not if you don't give her the chance to."

I hadn't even realized I'd spoken aloud.

"All I'm saying is"—Abby lifted the grilled cheese out of the skillet, added a second—"I'm very familiar with the feelings I see in Leah's eyes. Don't give up, Remi. If you do, you'll regret it for the rest of your life. And so will she."

I cleared away the damn lump in my throat. "Have I ever told you thank you?"

She glanced at me, eyes wide with surprise. "For what?"

I watched her add a third sandwich to the pan. "For loving my brother. For showing us how to be a family." Without our parents, we'd been lost, the three of us wandering around in the dark.

"Oh, Remi." One side of Abby's mouth lifted in a sad smile. "I didn't know how to be a family any more than you three did. I just reached for what I wanted."

I glanced up at the ceiling, wishing I could see all the way up to the two people I wanted more than anything in my life. Was it really that easy?

Abby finished the last sandwich, then assembled the tray with the food and drinks for three. She added oatmeal molasses cookies before pushing it across the island toward me. "Go get 'em, brother."

I looked from this woman who'd changed all our lives, to the tray, and back again. Then picked up the offering she'd provided in both hands and headed upstairs.

Chapter Nineteen

Leah —

I'd brought a backpack full of things for Brooke, including her favorite pink pajamas with the white unicorns dancing across them, their rainbow horns bright and colorful. Brooke welcomed the warm fabric against her goose-bumped skin after her bath, but she wasn't smiling. Watching her, I wondered how long it would be before either one of us smiled again.

"Come on, baby." I urged her across the room to the bed, pulling back the covers for her to climb in. "Let's get you warm."

"Will you brush my hair, Mommy?"

I'd just brushed the tangles out in the bathroom, but that wasn't what she meant. From the time she was little, Brooke had been soothed by long sessions with the brush running through her hair. She needed to be soothed now more than ever. And maybe I needed to soothe her.

A knock sounded at the door. Brooke jumped.

I gathered her close, choking up at the evidence of her fear. "It's okay. Nothing to be afraid of here, I promise." The scent of soap and sweet baby filled my nose, reminding me she was here, safe, with me. "Let me go see who it is."

Brooke clung a moment longer before reluctantly releasing me. Another knock sounded as I crossed the room.

"Just a sec!"

Opening the door allowed the scent of tomatoes and cheese and toasty bread to flow in, but it was the sight that greeted me that made me warm—Remi, a full tray gripped in his hands. That same sense of security flowed through me as I'd had with Brooke, the rightness of having him here with me. With us.

Was it right? I'd seen firsthand what this man was capable of, but tonight I really didn't care. I was listening to my heart, my head be damned.

"I thought you two might want some dinner." He shifted from one foot to the next, his eyes full of… I don't know. Something I'd never seen before, not on Remi. Something that only grew stronger when Brooke called my name.

I stepped back to let him in. "Thank you." Why hadn't I thought of this? I had no idea how long it had been since Brooke had a decent meal.

"Thank Abby," Remi whispered as he passed. "She sent cookies."

My laugh surprised me.

"Hungry, little one?" Remi asked. He crossed the room to a table in the corner, seeming oblivious to Brooke's absolute silence and wary gaze. "I hope you like grilled cheese."

Brooke was peeking over the blanket she'd pulled up to her face, following Remi's every move as he began laying out the food. I watched the tension seep into his body, and that's when I realized what I had seen earlier, flickering in his eyes—fear. Remi was afraid of a little girl.

He should be. Children cut through bullshit faster than any adult ever could, cut down to the truth of you in seconds, and they weren't afraid to reveal whatever they discovered. I needed to keep that in mind. Brooke realizing that Remi and I were close would have been my worst nightmare until today.

Having a gun held to your daughter's head, watching men bleed out in front of you—it all had a way of putting everything in perspective.

I crossed the room and pulled him toward the bed. "Brooke, this is my friend Remi."

His fingers twitched against mine as he waited for her response. Brooke stared at our entwined hands for a minute, still clutching the blanket. "You came with my mommy to the bad place."

Now it was my turn to flinch.

Remi went to his knees beside the bed. "I did. I came to help your mom." He held out his hand. "Hi."

The word was croaked, Remi's uncertainty lightening my heavy heart. I laid my palm on his broad back, felt him hold his breath as Brooke made her decision. Finally one tiny hand let go of the blanket and met Remi's. "Hi."

"Remi brought us some food," I said, hoping to give him a chance to breathe. "Come eat."

Brooke eased from the bed, still a bit wary. She'd always been like me—serious, careful, but with that friendly trust most kids had. She'd seen too much, had too much done to her in the past few days for that natural openness to not be damaged. Every time I thought about it, every time I saw the fear on her face, the urge to strangle Ross with my bare hands surged inside me. And then I'd remember that I couldn't because he was already dead, and grief would rush in to mix with the anger.

The roller coaster probably wasn't going to stop anytime soon, for me or for Brooke.

The tomato-and-cheese goodness filling the air actually drew a growl from my stomach. I made sure Brooke had all she needed, watched for her to take her first bite, then attacked my plate. Remi watched, a soft look on his face, as he ate his own food.

"Mommy, where is Mrs. Lydia?"

I paused, my spoon halfway to my mouth. I'd never lied to my daughter, but then I'd also never told her someone she loved was dead. "Lydia hurt her head badly, baby."

She looked up at me, eyes wide and shining, as if she knew what was coming but still had to ask. "Did the doctor fix it?"

He didn't have a chance. "They couldn't fix it, Brooke."

"She died?" A tear slid down Brooke's face.

I reached for her, took a deep breath. "She did. I'm so sorry, but she did."

"Did Uncle Ross die?"

He had told her he was her uncle? "He was hurt very badly too."

"By the bad man."

"Yes."

She pushed her spoon around in her soup. "Uncle Ross told me to be very quiet and we'd be okay. We had to stay quiet or the bad man would get angry."

Ross said he'd protected her. Was that what Brooke was saying?

"Why'd the bad man hurt him, Mommy?" More tears fell. "Will he come back? Will he hurt us too?"

I raised desperate eyes to Remi's. How did I answer that question?

"Brooke," Remi said, his voice low and firm. Something in me settled at that tone, just as he'd probably intended. "The bad man is not coming back, I promise you."

Don't promise. Don't make her believe something that might not be true.

But Remi wasn't listening. Laying his napkin on the table, he rose from his seat. "Come look at this."

I followed as Brooke scooted from her chair and walked with Remi across the room to the darkened window. Kneeling next to Brooke, he pulled the curtain aside. "See that gate way out there?" He pointed. "And that fence that goes as far as you can see?"

Brooke nodded.

"That gate keeps the bad man out. And we have cameras everywhere so we can see any bad men coming a mile away."

"What if they get in anyway?"

"They won't," Remi told her, the words absolutely certain. "And even if something bad happened, if someone tried to get in? They'll never get past me and my brothers."

Brooke frowned up at him. "What brothers? Are they as big as you?"

Remi grinned. "Almost." He flexed a bicep. "Do you think any bad guys could get past that?"

Brooke dared to poke the hard muscle with a finger. "No."

Remi gave her a sharp nod. "No is right."

And then my daughter did something I hadn't expected to see for a long time—she smiled. Not just a turning up of her lips, but a genuine smile that reached all the way to her eyes. Remi smiled too, and the oddest sensation filled me. Like my heart melted right into the floor and my ovaries exploded all at the same time.

Lethal. This man was lethal, in more ways than one, and I'd better remember that.

After we finished the cookies Abby had sent and gathered our dishes onto the tray, I put a couple of pillows on the floor in front of my chair for Brooke, bumping her up to the right height, and began long, soothing brushes through her hair as she leaned against my knee. Remi sat, watching us in the quiet. Gradually Brooke's weight became heavier and heavier against me until I knew she was asleep, her head lying on my thigh.

"You're a good mom, Leah," Remi said as I laid the brush aside.

"I try." That's all you could really do. When I'd discovered I was pregnant, I'd been terrified. My mom had died when I was little, and Angelo hadn't had any family. How was I supposed to know how to raise a child? But then I'd ended up on the run. At that point I figured I couldn't screw it up any worse, so I'd promised myself to try my hardest. Brooke and I had figured out the mother/daughter thing together.

"Not everyone does."

No, they didn't. I sifted my fingers through Brooke's honey-colored strands. "What about your parents?"

Pain flashed in his amber eyes, and I wished I'd bitten my tongue.

"They were the best, at least what little I remember. Kids have an amazing ability to forget things that aren't so perfect."

I hoped Brooke managed to forget some things from the past few days. "You were young when they died, right?" I thought I remembered that from the news coverage when they had taken over Hacr Technologies. "When your uncle sent you to boarding school?"

Remi huffed. "He didn't send us to boarding school. We ran away. Or rather, Levi took us away."

"What? Why?"

Remi raised his gaze from Brooke's sleeping form to meet mine, staring hard. "Because he'd killed my parents. And he would've eventually killed us."

"I thought they never caught your parents' killer." Or his uncle's.

"Levi witnessed the murder."

I closed my eyes and breathed out a curse. That one piece of information explained so much about Remi's brother.

"Where did you go?"

Remi shrugged. "There was nowhere to go. Nowhere safe."

"So…" I considered his words, the posture of his body. They'd run, but… "You lived on the streets."

"We took care of each other," he said, rising from his chair to gather the tray.

They'd had each other and no one else, no one to keep them safe. Not like Brooke. How had that affected them, three little boys surviving on their own? The streets were hard enough for adults, much less…

My stomach turned. "Remi—"

He was almost to the door. "You get Brooke in bed while I take this downstairs."

Something about the words made me hesitate. "You're not staying here tonight, Remi." The bed was big, but not big enough for three. Besides, I didn't want Brooke seeing Remi sleeping with me. There'd be too many questions I couldn't answer.

"I'm definitely staying here"—he opened the door before turning back to me—"right there in that chair." He jerked his chin toward a deep, plush armchair in the corner. "Brooke will wake up tonight. She'll be scared. And I'll be there to assure her she has a guard watching over her every minute."

There was that damn melting/ovaries exploding thing again. I really wished it would go away. Especially since this time it was mixed with a seeping disappointment that Remi wasn't staying for me.

Get a grip, Leah.

"Put her to bed," Remi was saying, seeming oblivious to the internal psychoses duking it out in my brain. "I'll be right back."

He moved to pull the door closed, then stuck his head back inside. "Oh, and Leah?"

"Yeah?"

"I expect a good-night kiss when I get back."

The door closed behind him. He couldn't have moved a step away, though, because when I let a curse loose, his laugh reached me before fading down the hall.

Chapter Twenty

Remi —

The crick in my neck had totally been worth it. For the first time in my life, I'd felt worthy. Powerful. I'd kept watch over the two females who meant everything to me, soothing away the nightmares with a few gentle words when either woke up, and this morning, despite feeling like shit from lack of sleep, I also felt like captain of the fucking universe. Like I had found the one thing I was meant to do for the rest of my life.

Now I just had to convince Leah to believe it too.

Letting myself out just before seven, I closed the bedroom door behind me and went to take a shower. Half an hour later I was working on breakfast for six. Six. Holy shit. How had our little family of three, relying on no one but each other, doubled in size so fast?

I almost asked Levi that when he followed me in, but kept my mouth shut, not quite ready to let his particular brand of logic become a downer this morning. Eli arrived shortly after, then Abby, meaning everyone was in the room when Leah walked in with Brooke.

My brothers stilled immediately, their eyes on Leah's little girl. I could read the same fear in their eyes that I'd felt yesterday, the same *holy shit, it's a tiny human! How the fuck do I handle this?* Followed almost immediately by *don't say the word* fuck, *damn it!* Why was a child so terrifying? Maybe it was because we knew how easy it was to screw up a kid. Maybe it was because it had been a couple of decades since we'd been allowed to be kids. Maybe it was because we couldn't predict their actions like we could some asshole looking through the scope of a Remington 700.

Either way, it was best to treat them like a Tyrannosaurus rex—don't move and maybe they won't see you.

"Hey, everyone," Leah said, leading Brooke by the hand.

A chorus of hellos had Brooke's step hitching as they approached the table. Steeling my courage, figuring Brooke had to get used to me sometime, I stepped in to give Leah a quick kiss on the lips. Her eyes went wide, darted to Brooke, but I wasn't going to hold back for her daughter's sake. Brooke wouldn't trust me if I lied, with words or actions.

"Good morning, little one." I held out my hand. "Would you like to meet my family?"

The word *family* seemed to settle Brooke's nerves, as if being related meant the others were safe too. That hadn't proved the case with Ross, necessarily, but it would with the people in this room. When Brooke slid her tiny hand into my enormous paw, I got that same feeling I'd had earlier, like my chest had puffed out to twice its normal size and my head would no longer fit through the door. She was trusting me. So fragile and innocent, and she was trusting *me*.

I had to clear my throat before I could get any words out. Standing before the table, I pointed to each person. "Brooke, this is Levi, my brother. And his girlfriend, Abby. And my younger brother, Eli. This is Brooke."

My brothers smiled and said hello while going pale, as if I was about to ask them to babysit or change shitty diapers. Ignoring their weirdness, Abby was out of her chair and around the table in a flash. "It's so great to meet you, Brooke," she said, dropping to her knees in front of the six-year-old. She held out a hand to shake. "I hope you slept well."

Thank fuck for the woman in our family.

Brooke placed her hand in Abby's. "No," she said quietly, solemnly, "but Remi watched over us."

Abby reached for something around Brooke's throat. "That's a very pretty locket. Did your mommy give that to you?"

I glanced down to see a delicate filigree heart-shaped locket lying just under the edge of Brooke's shirt. Abby pulled it out to admire.

"My daddy gave it to me," Brooke said confidently.

I jerked my gaze to Leah, holding my breath.

Leah's smile was sad. "Angelo gave it to me. It became Brooke's on her fifth birthday."

Angelo had given it to her? I went slowly to my knees, not wanting to startle Brooke. "It's beautiful," I told the girl. "Can I see?"

When Brooke nodded, I took the heart from Abby. The light danced on the silver surface, disappeared into the valleys of the delicate pattern. "I didn't see this last night."

Leah frowned. "I took it off for her bath. Brooke's allowed to wear it during the day. She had it on when…"

I nodded, understanding what she didn't say— that Brooke had the necklace around her neck when she'd been kidnapped. I fingered the catch on the locket but didn't feel any give. Using a nail, I pressed harder, finally rewarded with a small *snick*.

The locket popped open.

Brooke and Leah both gasped. Brooke took a step back, stopped by Leah's body behind her.

"It's all right," I said, easing my hand closer so the chain didn't pull on Brooke's neck. "Eli, come here." Heart pounding hard, I glanced up at Leah. "When did Angelo give this to you?"

"When…" Her voice shook. "When I found out I was pregnant."

I held her gaze as the gravity of her answer settled on my chest. Angelo, knowing the woman he loved, the woman who carried his child, needed security, had given her what he'd thought was the only security he could—the evidence against his employers. Because there, glistening inside the small heart, was a microchip. A chip that had hung around his daughter's neck while her kidnappers searched for the fucking thing everywhere but there.

Why the hell did the men I wanted to kill all have to be dead? Leah had carried the evidence on her body when she'd fled that night. Brooke had worn it for over a year, with no idea that the pretty necklace from her daddy could be either her salvation or a death sentence.

Jesus Christ, I wished I could kill the man all over again.

"Brooke, little one"—I dropped the heart, then tapped her chin playfully—"we need to borrow your pretty necklace a minute, please. Can Eli see it and bring it back to you in just few minutes."

A vee appeared between Brooke's eyes, making her look so much like Leah for a moment that I almost let a laugh escape. She glanced up at her mama, then back to me.

"Just for a minute; it's really important."

"He'll give it back, Brooke," Leah assured her.

Brooke finally nodded.

"Okay." Gently I lifted the necklace over her head. When I passed it to Eli, it was with the heart open, the chip plainly visible.

"I'll be right back." Eli winked at Brooke. "I promise." He sprinted from the room.

I helped Leah settle Brooke at the table. "How about a cinnamon roll and some eggs?"

Brooke's eyes lit up. "And bacon?"

Leah chuckled. "We both love our bacon, don't we?"

"Yes!" Brooke turned to me, eyes softening me up more than a puppy dog's ever could. "Please?"

I laughed. "I can see I'll have to up my bacon game. Turns out I do have some just waiting for you."

Brooke's smile made my chest go tight.

Eli was back before breakfast was over. He handed the necklace to me, and I slipped it over Brooke's head. She smiled at me again, this time around a big bite of bacon. Leah's gratitude shone from her eyes when I glanced up.

"I've got the"—Eli paused, eyed Brooke—"information downloading."

"I imagine you all have some planning to do," Abby said. "Maybe Brooke wouldn't mind helping me carry the dishes to the sink, and after I load the dishwasher, we could play Frogger."

Brooke looked to her mom as if for permission. When Leah nodded, she asked, "What's Frogger?"

Abby gasped. "What is Frogger? You mean you've never played Frogger?"

Brooke shook her head, smiling a bit at Abby's antics.

"You have been missing out, girlfriend." Abby stood and began to gather plates. "Frogger is only the best video game of all time! These guys play their zombie games—"

"Zombies?" Brooke's eyes rounded.

"Zombies! And race cars. And—" Abby waved off the rest of the list as if our RPGs were too silly to care about. "Give me the classic games anytime. And Frogger is the best of the classics."

Leah stood, watching Abby and Brooke carry dishes over to the counter. The uncertainty in her expression, the need to both be with her daughter and address the issues we both knew weren't going away, tore at me. I moved behind her, slid an arm around her hip to her stomach, ignoring the tensing of her body against me.

"She'll be fine with Abby for a little while," I said quietly. "And we'll be an easy intercom away if she needs anything at all."

Leah grabbed my wrist. "I don't know how to do this," she admitted, voice just as soft so that Brooke couldn't hear. "I'm a mom, not a…vigilante. I can't fight the mob."

"You're a stronger fighter than you will probably ever realize, *eshet hayil*. But this time you don't have to fight alone—we'll do it with you." I wanted to do it for her, but hard as it was for me to accept, I knew I couldn't. Leah needed to have some part in closing this door to her past.

I couldn't resist the pull of her warmth and bent to nuzzle the side of her neck. "Come downstairs and we'll work it out."

She turned into me, her hand coming up to grab my shirt, clutch it in her fist just over my heart. I covered it with my own.

"Okay," she finally said. "Let me tell her where I'll be, and we can go."

When she released me, a part of me went with her. I thought that might always be the case. Even if she walked away from me, we would always be connected. But my job was to convince her to stay; I just had to figure out how.

Chapter Twenty-One

Leah —

Brooke happily followed Abby to an office where an old-fashioned Atari setup waited. I was surprised the thing actually worked, but according to Eli, the refurbished classics were all the rage nowadays. I left Brooke to learn about Frogger and followed the men down to the bat cave.

Downstairs, we gathered around a small conference table that looked more like it belonged in an executive boardroom than the basement playground for three assassins. Remi sat next to me, his big body barely contained by the chair he squeezed himself into. I don't think that's why his arm and leg pressed against mine, though. That was because he wanted to torture me. His heat and scent reminded me that I'd woken up beside this man only twenty-four hours ago. I knew what he felt like when he was hungry for me, what he looked like in the grip of climax. I might be a mom, but I was also a woman, and now that Brooke was safe, I found myself remembering.

And wanting.

Ross just died. Your life is in chaos. You shouldn't be thinking about sex!

Why the hell not? Remi and Brooke were the only good things in my life right now.

The thought struck me right between the eyes. Remi was a good thing. He was. I trusted this man with my daughter's life, with my body. So what did that mean in the long run? Because I couldn't see myself married and raising a daughter with a man who killed people for a living. I could see myself walking away, knew in some part of my overloaded brain that it was the right thing to do, but just the thought made my heart ache so bad I had no idea how I'd go through with it.

When had it gotten this strong between us? And where did that leave me in the end?

"What are our options?" I asked, reaching for a distraction from the confusion building inside me.

"There are a few," Remi began.

"Not all of them good," Eli pointed out. "A full-on assault on the Fiori family, for instance."

Levi leaned back in his chair across the table from me. "We could certainly try, but the likelihood of catching every member of the family—"

"And anyone associated with them," Eli put in.

"Is nil." Remi rubbed at the scruff he hadn't bothered to shave this morning. He'd scraped that soft-sandpaper beard across my skin the night before last, left behind reddened patches on my neck and breasts still sensitized to his touch. The muscles low in my belly clenched at the memories the simple rasp of his palm over his chin brought forth. "Any vacancy we create will be filled almost immediately, either from within the family or outside it. Not a good option."

I tapped my finger on the armrest, willing my thoughts away from Remi and back on the task at hand. "Okay, so we can't kill them all." No matter how much I wanted that to be the plan. "What other options have we got?"

"We can go with the original plan and hand over the recordings," Eli suggested.

"I'm not sure that's a viable option either," Levi said, rocking in his seat like it was a rocking chair on the front porch. "That's what they demanded, but the more I think about it, the more I believe they never intended for anyone to walk out of that warehouse alive except Fiori's men. They wanted the recordings, yes. But they couldn't guarantee there were no copies. Couldn't guarantee Leah hadn't told anyone else about the evidence. They didn't make it clear to Ross, but this was a scorched-earth tactic from the get-go in my opinion."

A tactic that had taken the life of the only sibling I had. That had almost taken the life of my six-year-old child. As if watching it on a movie screen, I saw the moment Ross fell to the ground, saw his desperate hands tugging at the ropes to release Brooke before it was too late to save her. Anger rose in a noxious wave, roiling inside me, growing and growing and growing until there wasn't room to breathe, much less think.

And then a warm hand settled on my thigh. *Remi.* His palm opened, his long fingers circling my leg, gripping me. Grounding me. His touch centered me when I couldn't center myself, couldn't push away the pain. I didn't look at him, not with so many eyes watching, but I covered his hand with mine, keeping him close.

"So giving the recordings back isn't a good option. What is?" I asked, voice a rasp in my tight throat.

"What about your father?" Levi asked.

A rough growl escaped Remi's throat. I shot him a surprised glance.

"What about him?" I asked.

"Can he help us?"

I'd considered that and rejected it after Angelo's death, not wanting to pit him and Ross against each other. I'd lost the father of my child and my brother all at once; I'd decided I'd rather Dad be safe than at risk because of me. Now... "He's solid."

"Are you sure? Ross wasn't," Remi pointed out, his voice as rough as the sound that had escaped him. "What are the chances that your father was working both sides as well?"

The words were like a slap in the face. Was Remi blaming me for Ross's betrayal, for not seeing the truth sooner? I dared to meet those amber eyes, glowing with emotion, and realized the answer was no. He was angry—at Ross, at the situation—but that fierceness in his gaze... He wanted to protect me. Dad was an unknown to him.

I squeezed Remi's hand beneath mine. "I'm sure. If Dad had been working both sides, it wouldn't have mattered if he got ahold of the recording; he could make them disappear. Ross was the one who kept me from going to my dad back then."

The tension in Remi's body eased the slightest bit. Nothing would reassure him like meeting my father and seeing the truth for himself, but for now, he was choosing to trust me like I'd trusted him.

"Does he have the guts to stand up to the mob?" Levi asked.

"Yes." I truly believed that. Seven years ago I'd doubted my father's ability to take down his own son, not his willingness to take on the mob. "Still, even with the evidence we have—and what they'll hopefully gain once the recordings give them an opening—the cops won't catch everyone. There will be retaliation; it's a given. I don't want that for me or him or the men who work for him, but what other choice do we have?"

Remi and Levi exchanged a look, seeming to communicate without speaking. Did they have some ideas they weren't laying out on the table yet? Did I want to know what they were?

"Let's at least start with your dad," Levi finally said. "He knows all the local players. Between us, we should be able to figure out the next step."

I wasn't sure how I felt about seeing Dad again, coming back from the dead, so to speak. I'd forced myself to walk away, not look back. To give up any hope of ever returning to the life I'd once known. I doubted the reality would hit me until I was face-to-face with the man who'd raised me, loved me. Could we have that back? Would he blame me for Ross's death?

I didn't know. Right now reuniting with my family had to come second to stopping the Fioris. They'd taken the father of my child, my brother, had almost taken my daughter from me. They'd stolen my life. They had to be stopped.

And looking around the table, I knew I trusted these three men to help me do that. As long as I was a part of whatever plan they finally decided on, and Brooke was safe in the end, I would trust them. I knew Remi and his brothers would choose the wisest course. But...

"We'll be going to DC?"

Remi nodded.

"I won't leave Brooke behind." Not right now, when her equilibrium was fragile and her fear could rear its ugly head at any moment. She had to be with me. If that meant traveling, we'd roll with it.

But Remi seemed to have anticipated that as well. "I think we might have a way to take her with us and keep her safe at the same time," he said. Then to his brothers, "What about bringing in our new friends? They could be strong allies if we let them."

"Do assassins have allies?" I asked, only partly teasing.

"Not in the business," Eli said with a wink. My heart lifted the tiniest bit.

"But we can go outside the business," Remi added. "It's actually safer that way."

"Who would you trust?" Remi wouldn't trust just anyone, not with Brooke's safety at risk; I truly believed that. And then the pieces began to assemble themselves into a logical answer. "King?"

"His team is the best JCL has." Levi shifted in his seat, the move clueing me in that he wasn't as comfortable with outsiders as Remi was. Being the oldest, the one responsible for his family when they'd been on the streets, that didn't surprise me. "As much as an outside firm is never my first choice, we can't both handle the mob and keep Brooke safe. Knowing what I know about King's team, I do believe they can protect her."

Levi didn't give his trust easily. I nodded my agreement.

"I'll get on the arrangements," Eli said, rising from his seat.

I watched Remi's brothers as they crossed the room to the bank of computers we'd used the first time Remi had brought me down here, unsure how I felt. Relieved, like someone had taken the burden from my shoulders, broken it into pieces, and scattered it among the four of us so I didn't have to carry it all on my own. And yet still anxious because we didn't know what would happen when we got to DC. I turned to Remi—

And realized he was watching me, the same mix of emotions in his gaze. And a message: *We'll figure it out.*

I wasn't alone.

Tears pricked the backs of my eyes.

"Let's go upstairs, leave these two to the details," he said. The words had a rough undertone that slid beneath my anxiety and touched a different part of me, a part that had been put on the back burner since we'd gotten out of bed yesterday. A part that surged to the fore with a suddenness that shocked me.

"Upstairs." I squeezed my thighs together, only then realizing that Remi's fingers had curled along my inner thigh, so close to the spot that needed him the most. "All right."

His grin was wicked enough to curl my toes. "Upstairs, *lev sheli.*"

Chapter Twenty-Two

Remi —

Lev sheli. My heart. That's what Leah was. That and so much more.

I kept her hand in mine as we walked toward the elevator. Abby and Brooke were on the ground floor, and we'd join them there...in a little bit. First, I needed time with Leah, needed to wipe that lost, scared look away, the one I'd caught far too often staring back at me. I needed to take her away, just for a little bit, give her some semblance of peace—if she'd let me.

The doors opened, then closed behind us. I eyed Leah as I pushed the button for the third floor.

"Brooke was with us last night," I said, watching her eyes widen when she noticed our destination. "She'll be with us on this trip." Along with my brothers and the four members of King's team if we could get them.

Leah frowned. "Does that bother you?"

"Hell no, it doesn't bother me." That was part of being a parent, right? Having a kid limit the possibility of sex was a given; that didn't make your sex life nonexistent. "It just means we have to take advantage of an opportunity when it presents itself."

I pushed the emergency stop button, bringing the elevator to a halt between floors.

"Oh."

That one little syllable and my dick went hard as a rock. I grinned. "Oh."

I didn't have a lot of room to maneuver, so it took me about two seconds to stalk her across the tiny elevator car. Long enough for Leah's eyes to go dark, drowsy. To get that sexed-up look I'd had to mostly imagine in the dark the other night. Now there was no hiding the slightest nuance of her expression. There would be no hiding the smallest centimeter of her body either.

I reached for the top button on her shirt. Her skin began to flush and her breath quickened as I flicked the buttons open one by one, revealing inch after inch of creamy, silken skin that made my mouth water with anticipation. The last one undone, I moved to the closure of her jeans, then the zipper. And then I grasped the waist and pulled, going to my knees to remove her pants and give me the access I was dying for.

A loud *buzz* filled the car. Leah startled, goose bumps jumping across her skin.

"Remi, take whatever you're doing out of the elevator."

Levi. Fucking bastard. He knew exactly what I was doing.

"Please tell me there aren't cameras in here," Leah whispered.

I laid my palms against her ankles and swept them slowly up her legs, absorbing the heat and feel of her. "No cameras," I said roughly, then louder. "Piss off, bro!"

"Get out of the elevator, dickhead." Eli this time.

I snorted a laugh. "Take the stairs, *dickhead*."

Leah choked out a laugh of her own, one that strangled to a stop when my hands slid under her panties to cup her ass. Such a full, firm ass. I leaned forward to place a kiss on the soft pillow of flesh just below her belly button.

"Remi—"

Clenching my fingers around handfuls of flesh, I let my sigh brush across Leah's mound. "Either piss off or you'll find the elevator out of commission for a lot longer than I'll be in here. Got me, bro?"

Leah dug into my hair, pushing deep to scrape her nails along my scalp. I barely held back a moan. Two grumbling voices came through the speakers, muttering threats and complaints and things I stopped paying attention to when Leah shimmied in my grasp, rubbing her ass harder into my hands. Sliding reluctantly away, I skidded across the floor on my knees and clicked off the intercom. "Drop those panties for me, Leah."

There was nothing choked about her laugh this time. "I bet you've made plenty of panties drop in your life, Remi."

"And yours are the only ones that matter," I told her honestly. Whether she believed me or not, my cock had never been hard enough to hammer nails with anyone but her. I held my breath and watched as her fingers pushed at the silk wrapped around her hips. It whispered softly as it slid down her skin to her ankles, where she kicked them into the corner along with her jeans. I was between her legs before she could close them again.

"Open for me, *lev sheli.*" Palms on her inner thighs, I pushed out until the soft folds I hungered for parted.

"Remi." Leah pulled at my hair again, urging me forward. "God, please."

"Please what?" I asked, mouth and breath brushing her most private skin.

"Please suck me."

I stroked my thumbs along the creases between thigh and hip, tugged her lips open even farther. And when that tiny bud poked its head out, ready to play, I sucked it into my mouth and pressed hard with my tongue.

Leah's knees went weak.

Oh no, you're not going anywhere.

Forcing myself closer, I ate at her pussy, sucking and biting and laving and rubbing. Cream filled my mouth; the wild, spicy scent of her filled my nose. I wanted her climax, wanted to feel her clenching around my tongue and strangling on her own breath, and I chased that goal with everything I had in me. Her hips tilted, letting me thrust inside her, letting my tongue slide along her clit with every withdrawal before pushing forward again. I trailed my fingers along the crease of her ass, heard her strangled gasp when I circled the tightly closed bud that hid there. When I pressed against it, Leah cried out my name, shock and heat filling her voice.

She didn't stop me; instead she rolled her hips against my face, widened her legs, opened herself to me completely. And I took everything she gave, pushing hard to give her more. When her legs began to tremble and her cream flooded my mouth, I pushed a finger just barely into the opening I knew, without doubt, was virgin, and felt her fly apart on my tongue.

I was pushing back, tearing at my fly the very next second.

"Come here, *lev sheli*." Propping my back against the wall, I dug a condom out of my pocket. "Come to me, love."

Leah shrugged out of her shirt as I watched, still struggling to catch her breath. Spasms rippled along her belly, and my cock jerked, wept, needing to feel them along my skin. Fuck, I needed her riding my dick now, not ten seconds from now. "Leah!"

A secretive smile crossed her lips. One slow step at a time, she crossed to me, unhooking her bra along the way. "What does *lev sheli* mean, Remi?" Her breasts swayed as she sucked in a breath. "Tell me."

God, I wasn't sure I could. I wasn't sure I could do anything but beg for her to get down on my lap and shove me deep inside her body. "Leah." I swallowed hard. "Fuckin' A, hurry up."

"Hurry? There's no hurry, is there?" She dropped slowly to her knees, crawled up my legs. "No one needs the elevator. Brooke is taken care of. There's no reason to hurry."

I cupped her breasts where they fell from her body. They were the perfect fit for my big hands, her nipples the perfect fit for my mouth. "Come up here and let me fuck you."

"Not yet," she whispered, then dipped her head to my cock. A shout left me as her lips surrounded my erection. When she sucked, the first spurt of my orgasm escaped into her mouth.

I hissed, reaching down to squeeze the base of my cock. "Damn it, woman, get up here."

Leah licked me from top to bottom, then up again. "Did you need something?"

I needed to pound us both into oblivion was what I needed. Except I couldn't catch my breath enough to say it. Instead I growled my displeasure while arching to get my cock closer to her mouth.

She opened over me and sucked me to the back of her throat—and I lost it. Every filthy curse I'd ever known left me along with my come and my self-control. Never had I climaxed before I was ready to. Never had I given a woman my sperm until I decided it was time. But this wasn't any woman—it was Leah, and she wrung every drop from me without my permission or my regret. I gave her every last drop I had.

And then dragged her onto my lap and impaled her on my still-hard, aching cock.

"Fuck!" Lifting her body, I forced the condom over my skin, then pushed back inside her. Only then could I hold myself still, come to some semblance of control, with her body gripping mine like a steel vise.

"We've got to stop doing that," Leah said softly, breathlessly in my ear. Opening her legs a fraction more allowed me in deeper, and we both groaned as my cock head pushed as far as it could go and her body gripped me all the way to the root.

"Maybe we should consider the pill," I whispered.

Yeah, right. Why would this woman, the one my family had kidnapped, the one I'd stalked, who'd had her daughter taken and her brother murdered, ever consider fucking someone like me skin to skin on purpose? But God, I wanted it. I wanted her body gripping me with no barrier between us. I wanted to take her without a condom or even the pill. I wanted my come inside her, taking root, giving me something

I'd never thought I'd have—acceptance. A permanent place in this world, the only place I'd ever wanted: by her side.

I buried my face in her neck and waited for her to reject me.

Leah circled her hips, the pleasure so great my fingers dug into her hips in response.

"Maybe we should," she whispered.

"Leah." I lifted her up, dropped her down on my cock. She let gravity do its work, slamming her onto me, smashing her clit against my pubic bone. "Don't."

"Don't what?" she asked as I did it again. "Don't what, Remi?"

I worked her over me, desperate to bring us both to another peak. "Don't give me hope when you don't mean it."

She laughed, the sound rough, raspy, as she labored along with me. "I don't know what I have to give anymore," she told me, "except this." She squeezed down hard on the ride up, forcing my breath out of my body. "Me." Flooding my cock on the ride down. "Now." Circling her hips when I hilted.

"Fuck, fuck, fuck." The curse became a chant as I let go of logic and thought and chased the pleasure drowning my every cell. I opened my eyes to see Leah's breasts right there, waiting for me, the tight strawberry-red tips begging me for attention. And I gave it. Catching her nipple between my teeth, I closed my lips and sucked hard—once, twice. Ground her body down on my cock.

And felt her climax rock through her pelvis. Seconds later, the spasms took me with her.

Chapter Twenty-Three

Leah —

We drove to Atlanta Regional after dark. Turned out Hacr Technology had their own private jet, which the owners—the Agozis—had access to. Remi parked the Expedition next to a large hangar, the bright lights lining the outside illuminating a plane on the tarmac. The steps were already down, and five people stood at the base, waiting.

"Mommy?"

Brooke's voice had that strained tone I knew all too well, the one that said she'd moved from *I'm accepting all of this okay no matter how many new things come at me* to *one more thing and I'm going to lose it big-time, Mommy*. Every mother knew that tone. Honestly I was surprised she'd made it this far. We'd lain down for a nap after lunch, trying to get a little bit of a break, but Brooke hadn't slept for more than a few minutes at a time before waking from bad dreams.

I reached for her hand. "Yeah, baby?"

Her gaze was on the jet a hundred yards away. "Are we going on that?"

We'd never flown before. I was a little nervous myself. What was it everyone said when you were flying, that it was safer than driving? My mind understood the statistics, but my emotions screamed that at least when I was driving, I had control of the wheel. Still, wasting hours driving to DC was a ludicrous idea.

I knew that. Didn't stop me from feeling a bit queasy at the thought of walking up those steps and strapping myself into a metal tube.

Remi opened my door. "We are, little one," he said, answering for me.

I cleared my throat. "We haven't gotten to ride in an airplane before."

The words were scratchy despite my efforts to smooth them. Remi had to realize I was scared—of this, of what came next, of the chaos my life had become. It was all jumbled up together, and like Brooke, what I really wanted to do was lose it big-time. Probably the only reason I hadn't was those few minutes in the elevator this morning. And just like then, I reached for the man who'd become my lifeline.

A strong, solid hand closed around mine. When I looked up at Remi, understanding stared back at me. I hoped my strained smile conveyed how grateful I was before I turned to click open the seat belt strapping Brooke into her booster seat. Remi had produced the thing from thin air when we left the mansion, just another small touch in a sea of touches to be thankful for.

Brooke slid out of the booster, then crowded back against the driver's seat. "I don't wanna go, Mommy."

Behind us, Eli and Abby exited the back seat, while Levi got out of the front. Abby had insisted on accompanying us, pointing out that we might have to be gone for extended periods of time, and Brooke would be more comfortable during those times with a familiar face. Another thing I was grateful for. This family had come with more surprises—and more blessings—than I'd thought possible.

I held out a hand to Brooke. "I know it's something new, Brooke. It may seem scary." God knows I understood that. "But it's perfectly safe, baby. Mommy wouldn't take you on an airplane if it wasn't."

Brooke glanced from the plane to me and back again, and to my horror, tears gathered in her eyes and began to run down her cheeks. "No, Mommy! I don't wanna go. I don't wanna fly!"

Sympathetic tears burned at the back of my eyes. "Baby—"

"No!"

The sobs came then. Brooke crumpled onto the floorboard of the truck, huddled in the corner, the sight tearing at my mama heart until my own tears fell. "Brooke, love..." Instinctively I turned to Remi—me, who'd never relied on anyone, even Lydia, in handling my child. The knowledge added to my own overwhelm. "Remi..."

He glanced from me to Brooke, no impatience, not even a hint of disapproval visible. Remi didn't seem to care if a jet and eight people waited for us. He laid his warm hand on my back and rubbed the length of my spine. "It's been a helluva long day for all of us, but especially you two. How about giving us a minute?"

"But—" No. This was my job; I was the mom. I glanced at Brooke, lost in her tears, then Remi, and back. What did he know about soothing a crying child? "I have to—"

I turned back to Remi...and stopped. The gleam of his amber eyes in the dark, the sympathy in his expression, the relaxed stance of his body. Remi had been raised on the streets with no mother and no father. He'd had a younger brother who'd probably needed a lot of patience and care. Levi'd had the job of providing for them; what had Remi done?

I'd trusted him to rescue my child. Why couldn't I trust him to take care of her?

Would Brooke hate me for walking away?

I swear I almost rolled my eyes at myself. "Okay."

Stepping out of the Expedition, I forced my feet to take me across the tarmac toward the plane. My head kept tugging me back, but my heart said this was the right thing. I didn't allow myself to look back until I was approaching the crowd at the stairs. Remi sat in the open door of the truck, one leg casually drawn up, facing forward, his lips moving—talking to Brooke but not touching her. Waiting for her to come to him.

Emotion detonated in my chest as I watched him, so strong I stopped in my tracks. I hadn't wanted love since Angelo, hadn't dared risk someone knowing who I really was, opening myself up to someone. But now, with Remi... I knew this feeling. What I didn't know was what to do about it. I was in love with a man who could take a life without blinking. A man who was voracious in his need of me and, at the same time, took care of me in a way no one had in years. He was playful and sweet, and yet incredibly patient and tender with an overwhelmed six-year-old. I didn't understand the dichotomy in him, but I knew, without a doubt, that I wanted to. I wanted Remi in our lives.

Was that what he wanted when this was all over? And how would that work?

"Leah."

I turned to Levi, leaving the questions behind for now. The group waiting at the stairs greeted me as I joined them. King took the lead, pointing out our pilot, who retreated inside the plane, and then turning to his team. "JCL was kind enough to take me off desk duty a week early to accompany you. Don't worry; I don't need to kick ass with Elliot around."

A young blonde woman punched him in the arm, hard. I had to laugh; King Moncrief was the ultimate GQ model standing there in his crisp button-down and sport coat, and this woman was throwing punches at him. The size difference didn't help— Elliot was tiny compared to her teammates. Dressed in fatigues and a fitted leather jacket, she looked like she could hold her own—and handle the weapon strapped to her thigh—but against men the size of Remi and his brothers, or her own teammates? The three men were as different as night and day, but all of them rivaled the Agozis in size.

"He's not wrong," Elliot said as if she could read my mind. "Don't let my size fool you; I've taken all of these guys down on the mat." She jerked a thumb at her teammates.

"We don't typically start off a professional relationship comparing dick sizes, ma'am," an older man said, extending his hand to me. "Dain Brannan. I'm the head of this motley crew."

His handshake was firm, his gaze steady, instilling confidence. "Thank you for coming."

"Of course." He pointed to the members of his team. "You know King, I gather. This is Elliot Smith, and the quiet one over there actually behaving himself—very unusual—is Saint Solorio."

I shook hands with each of them, staring directly into their eyes. These were the people I was trusting with my daughter's life. Were they worthy of that trust? Would they protect her with their lives?

"You'll be with my daughter most of the time," I began. Dain raised a hand to stop me.

"She comes first, ma'am. Always. We have personal experience with a variety of situations, including"—he glanced at Elliot—"protecting a young child against immediate violent threats. Your daughter will be safe, I promise you."

I appreciated the assurances, but I didn't know them. I'd feel better if she was with Remi or his brothers, but that was impossible. Still, I nodded. "Thank you."

The team filed into the plane, Eli going with them. I turned to see Remi crossing the tarmac with Brooke in his arms. My daughter had her head on his shoulder, her little hands clutching his shoulders like a lifeline. I watched them approach, love surging so hard and fast it made my heart hurt.

"We just needed to catch our breath, Mommy," Remi said when he got close. "Right, little one?" He turned so I could see Brooke's face.

I reached up to brush the hair back from her eyes. "Okay?"

"I'm scared, Mommy. But Remi says it's okay to be scared."

"It is." She'd had so many scary things coming at her the past few days. I couldn't ask her to be brave again. I leaned close so only Brooke and Remi could hear me. "Wanna hear a secret? I'm a little scared too.

Being on an airplane is a brand-new thing, and brand-new things can be scary. But we'll get through it together, okay?"

A lingering tear trailed down her cheek to wet Remi's shoulder. My mommy instinct had me reaching up to wipe my baby's nose for her. Brooke jerked back, just like every child in the history of parenthood has done.

"Mommy!"

I laughed, a little watery. "Okay?"

She gripped Remi tighter as if he could give her courage. "Okay."

"Ready?" Remi asked.

"Ready." We walked toward the stairs, and Remi took my hand. I glanced down at our entwined fingers and wondered how I would ever go back to doing things on my own, without this man at my side. Because with him there, I felt like we could conquer anything that came our way.

Chapter Twenty-Four

Remi —

Eli had booked us into a hotel off the beaten path on the Virginia side of DC. My brothers and I were waiting when Leah exited the bedroom into the living area of one of the suites we'd commandeered.

"She's asleep?" I asked, noting the dark circles under Leah's eyes, the strain she couldn't hide. Brooke's pain was taking a toll. Dealing with the rest of this bullshit while being the best damn mother I'd ever known was sure as hell hard to handle. My arms ached to gather her up just like I'd gathered Brooke into them at the airport, to become the guard standing between her and the rest of the world. Some things, though, Leah needed to do herself, and tonight was one of those things.

"Yeah." She pushed the heavy fall of her hair back from her face. "Elliot sat with us while we read a book so Brooke could get used to her. She has a stepdaughter close to that age." Her gaze darted to Abby where she stood talking to Levi. "I still want Abby with her in case she wakes."

"She'll take good care of her, Leah. You know she will."

Frustration roughened her voice. "Of course she will. The point is, she's not me. I should be with my daughter, but I'm stuck cleaning up Ross and Angelo's fucking mess."

I did take her in my arms then, because I couldn't stand not to. Her smaller frame against mine made that protective instinct surge even stronger, and I curled myself around her, blocking out the rest of the world to give her a moment, however short, where it couldn't crowd in and tear her in any more directions than it already had.

"I'm just tired," she mumbled against my chest.

"So that's no to sex when we get back, right?" I asked, hoping for a smile.

Instead she nipped my pec, drawing a totally embarrassing yelp from me.

"Definitely a no," I confirmed, laughing.

"What the hell was that?" Eli asked behind me.

I groaned against the top of Leah's head. "See what you started? You've made me look like a pussy in front of my brothers. I'm gonna have to get my revenge later."

She raised her head, her gaze lighter, an almost smile on her lips. "I regret nothing."

I wanted to make her smile forever. Unfortunately, if things went south tonight, I might end up killing her dad—and that wasn't a metaphorical killing. She'd never smile at me again.

Levi had offered to do it earlier. He knew what it might cost me to take out a family member, what it might do to any relationship I hoped to have with Leah in the future. But this was my responsibility. If it came to that, I'd put him down easy. I was fucking praying like I'd never prayed before that Ross Windon, Sr had nothing to do with the Fiori family and Leah wouldn't lose another man to this nightmare. She deserved that.

"We need to go."

I acknowledged Levi's statement with a nod. "Let me check in with the team; then we can head out." Leaning down, I gave Leah a hard and fast kiss. "Go with Levi. I'll be a minute."

She threw an anxious look toward the bedroom door, her gaze trailing over the three men standing at various points around the room before moving back to me.

"She's going to be fine," I assured her again. I'd say it a million times if that's what it took to make her believe it.

"I know that in my head." Leah stepped back from my arms, leaving me feeling empty. "I guess a little separation anxiety is normal after what we've been through."

For both of us. I crossed my arms over my chest, pulling myself together. Pulling my emotions back behind the armor that protected me when I was on a job. Levi was the emotionless one; Eli the laid-back one. I'd thought throughout my teen years that something was wrong with me, that I felt too deeply, needed too much. It had taken me years to learn to manage my emotions, build the barriers that protected me from feeling so fiercely, but Leah... She blew those walls apart with a look, a touch.

I needed the walls back for now.

"It is normal," I said. "Go with Levi."

Dain moved toward me when I turned his way. "We have security set up, alarms and cameras. Eli has the codes for when you return. Saint and I will patrol regularly, Elliot will stay in the room with Brooke, and King will monitor everything from here."

I hadn't expected to like King's team, though I respected them. Dain had the kind of solid presence that very few men had, a quiet power that told you he knew what he was doing, knew his own strengths and weaknesses. I wouldn't trust anyone else with Leah's daughter. I also wouldn't tell him what we were doing. Dain and King—and, I assumed, the rest of his team—were straight-and-narrow men and women, and though they might agree with taking out the enemy, I doubted they'd approve of our methods. "We'll be back in a few hours. Fiori's men shouldn't be aware of our location, but don't get caught with your guard down."

"We won't." He stuck out a hand to shake. "Good hunting."

I certainly hoped it was.

Downstairs I made my way to the garage and the black SUV we'd rented. Eli drove, Levi in the front seat. After changing into the driver's uniform Eli had found from somewhere, I sat quietly in the back with Leah, waiting as Eli circled and backtracked, making sure we didn't have a tail. Finally, half an hour later, he headed for the location to pick up the car we'd arranged for me to drive.

"I don't understand why I can't go with you to pick him up," Leah finally said, voice hushed in the dark.

Studying all the possibilities, we'd decided Windon's house could be under surveillance, especially since the Fioris had to know Ross and their team were dead by now. I wouldn't risk Leah being seen there, so the plan changed to picking Windon up and bringing him to us. Luckily Eli had discovered a ball was being held tonight, some annual fundraiser Windon usually attended. He ordered a car service for formal events, Leah had told us. I would be the one driving Windon's town car tonight.

"You do understand," I said, knowing how smart Leah was. She got it; she was just struggling to accept it. "I'll bring him to you safe and sound."

"No stopping for a little side torture?" she asked. It might be dark, but I could tell from her voice she was only half kidding.

"We don't torture family," Eli cut in from the front as he pulled to a stop next to a black town car under a bridge in the middle of nowhere.

Leah shook her head. "I'm not family."

Levi glanced at her over his shoulder. "Right." He jerked his chin toward me. "In that case, just make sure he's still breathing when you show up."

"What?"

My brother winced at Leah's shriek.

"He's kidding," I assured her.

"Then he should learn to fucking smile every once in a while," she snarled.

Levi laughed. "I can when I want to, you know." He sobered. "And you are family, whether you want to acknowledge it or not. But even family isn't safe if they threaten the people we love."

And my brothers knew I loved Leah; there'd been no hiding it once she was with me.

"Get out, bro," Levi barked at me.

I took Leah's chin in my hand and brushed her mouth with mine. There was nothing I could say that would reassure her; best to just show up with her father intact—that would convince her far better than any words I could utter. "Later, *lev sheli.*"

I forced myself out of the truck before my walls cracked too much.

Downtown DC traffic was a bitch at any time, but on a weekend night... I found a place to hole up and waited for the call I knew was coming. Eli had managed to hack Windon's cell, rerouting any calls to the car service to his phone. When my brother's text came in, I made my way through traffic to the location, got out, and waited for my prey to arrive.

Ross Windon, Sr walked through the revolving door of the upscale hotel where the ball had taken place with a steady step, still fit after years behind a desk. I could see the resemblance to Leah immediately—the eyes, the mouth—but it was his son that he most resembled. Hair a bit grayer, more wrinkles around the eyes, but he was Ross Jr to a T. I opened the back door of the town car. "Sir."

A vee appeared between the man's brows. "Russell is off tonight."

Windon's regular driver. "Family emergency, sir. He sends his apologies."

"Hmm."

The man had good instincts. Something seemed off to him, I could tell. But he settled himself in the back seat nonetheless. Maybe desk duty had softened him a bit more than I'd realized.

I circled the car and got behind the wheel again. Windon was already pulling off his tuxedo jacket, seeming as anxious to get out of his monkey suit as I was to get out of this driver's uniform. Both of us would be disappointed for a few more hours.

Following the route the driver would typically take, I watched for a tail. If we were right and the Fioris were watching Windon, they'd put a serious damper on any interrogation—and cause a lot more cleanup than we had planned. Only when I was certain no one was following us did I deviate from the route and head toward the outskirts of town.

"Where are we going?" Windon asked. Not anxious, not yet. This was a man used to tense situations, used to threats.

"We're going to meet someone who needs to talk to you."

"Someone? That doesn't tell me anything. Who do you work for?"

A glance in my rearview showed the man's brows screwed together, his eyes narrowed as he stared back at me. "I work for myself, Commissioner Windon. The question is, who do you work for?"

"What the hell are you talking about? I work for this city!"

"So did your son," I pointed out. "That didn't stop him from finding another boss."

Windon went still, something like fear flickering in his expression. Not for him, I didn't think; he didn't appear to be that kind of man. For his son.

"Did? Didn't?" Tension radiated from him now, and I was thankful for the security at the ball, ensuring he wasn't armed at the moment. At least, we didn't think so. "Where is my son? Who the hell are you?"

"That, I can't tell you, not yet. But rest assured, it's a story you want to hear." I saw his mouth open, knew he was about to argue, and cut him off. "Sir, I'm not planning to hurt you. I'm not kidnapping you."

He snorted.

"Okay"—I gave him a smile that more resembled a shark than a friendly overture—"I am a little."

"Can you kidnap someone only a little?"

"Depends on how you look at it." I turned down a nondescript street leading into a quiet warehouse district. "You want to go to this meeting. And when it's over, I'll take you right back to your empty mansion in your wealthy neighborhood where you can sit in the silence and think about what you've learned. Don't make me force you. Just sit back and listen." I glanced at the nearest road sign. "We're almost there."

"Almost where?" He squinted out the window. "Meeting with whom?"

"You'll see."

Chapter Twenty-Five

Leah—

I'd grown up in the DC area, and I still had no clue where we were. Some abandoned office building in a run-down part of town. I guess when you needed space for illicit meetings, it paid to know what was off the beaten path, so to speak.

Standing here in the dark did nothing to stop the shivers rippling through me. In just a few minutes my father would arrive, see me, putting part of his world back together—right before I ripped it apart again. I still couldn't truly comprehend that my brother was gone. When I'd first run away, I'd find myself turning ten times a day to tell him or my dad something, share something that had happened, only to find they weren't there. Ross would never be there again.

The little bit of light from a partially uncovered window showed me Remi's brothers leaning casually against broken furniture, seeming completely content. Eli watched the window. Levi's focus was on his phone, the tracking program there giving him Remi's location in real time. I wanted to beg to see it. I wanted the shaking to stop. I wanted to stomp my foot and pace around to relieve the tension making it hard to draw a lungful of air, but I didn't. I couldn't. I was about to reveal myself to my father, who thought I'd run away, maybe even that I was dead, for seven years. Seven years. Longer than Brooke had been alive.

Having her snatched from me, I could now imagine all too well what my father had felt. My stomach bundled up in knots of agony just thinking about it.

"Relax, Leah," Levi growled, not taking his eyes from the screen. "Just relax."

"How the hell am I supposed to do that?" I snapped. Then sighed. This wasn't Levi's fault. It was mine. "I'm sorry."

He looked up then, the strange silver of his eyes glistening with the reflection from his phone. "For what? Being human. We are too. We get it."

A growl of my own rose in my throat. "Then why tell me to relax?"

Eli chuckled over by the window. "To make you feel inadequate. It's what he does." He waved a hand at his brother. "He needs to find some way of keeping us all below his level. He might say he's human, but he's more of an emotionless robot who expects nothing less from the rest of us."

The gleam of Eli's teeth told me he was smiling, but not too long ago I'd have been totally serious in agreeing with him. The first time I'd met Levi... A different kind of shiver shook me just thinking about it.

Levi shot his brother the bird. "Whatever, dickhead." Turning to me, he seemed to sober despite his lack of expression. "Just remember, not many people get a chance to do what you're about to do. Some people would kill for it."

Like him? Would Levi kill to be able to bring his parents back to life?

I imagined all the brothers would. I couldn't blame them.

"Besides"—Eli shifted so his back was to the wall—"if Windon isn't ecstatic to have his daughter back from the dead, we can always shoot him and put him out of his misery."

"What?"

Eli responded to my shout with a low snicker. "Hey, we do come in handy occasionally."

I just bet. I opened my mouth, ready to blast the sarcastic pain in the ass for scaring me, but choked back the words as the lights of a car flashed through the window. Both brothers went immediately on alert.

"Levi?"

He pocketed his phone. "It's him. Don't worry."

Less than half a minute passed before the door near Eli's now-covered window opened. It was only then that I realized the brothers had faded into the darkness, out of my line of sight. I held my breath and waited for the two men outside to enter the room.

The door clicked shut. The overhead lights switched on.

I blinked through the blinding brightness, my sight slowly adjusting until I could make out the man standing just a few feet inside the door. Tall, just like I remembered, though older and grayer. My father had always been what some would call distinguished, and time had only added to that, though the more I looked, the more I could see the edges of grief and pain in his face. I waited, shaking so hard now that my teeth chattered, until his eyes focused and found me across the room.

"Leah?"

"Dad," I whispered, unable to put more strength behind the word. I straightened, reached out for him. "How are you?"

My father crumpled to his knees.

The sound of sobs froze me in place. Shaking it off, I rushed forward, only to be stopped by Remi's forearm blocking my path. Keeping me from my father. I kept going.

"It might not be safe, Leah," Remi warned.

Fuck that. "He's my father." I struggled in Remi's hold. "You can kill him later, but let me go."

The hard arm across my middle slowly withdrew, and then I was on my knees beside my dad, gathering him into my arms. The next few minutes were a blur; I rocked him, reassured him, wept alongside him as the pain of the past seven years leached out of me. Maybe out of him. I'd only ever seen him cry at my mother's funeral, so long ago it was a vague memory, but now he wept as if releasing his soul, and I held him through it, feeling my own knit back together.

"Leah, my God." He finally raised his head, dark eyes staring, bewildered, into mine. "I can't believe it. I searched everywhere...God, how I searched for you." He glanced around the room, at Eli and Levi and Remi, and his muscles tensed beneath my hands. "Is this...did they take you?" Shaking hands pulled me closer to his body. "Did they keep you away from us?"

Before Remi could lose his shit—and I knew he would—I cupped my father's face and turned his attention back to me. "No, Dad. It wasn't them."

"Then who was it? Who took you? Where have you been?"

I did look to Remi then, unsure how to explain something so fraught with pitfalls. Eyes narrowed on us, Remi jerked his chin toward a couple of chairs we'd found intact. They were conveniently placed in the middle of the room, allowing the brothers easy access should any threat present itself.

"Leah?"

I turned back to my dad. "Come sit down."

He stood slowly, showing his age, or maybe that was the weight of the past few years. I was twenty-four; he was only in his late fifties. Nowhere near retirement. And yet he'd been through the loss of his beloved wife and teenage daughter. And now I would take his son from him as well. My chest ached so hard I struggled to breathe.

"What happened? Who are these men? Where have you been? Are you all right?"

The barrage of questions almost made me smile. I remembered this, the "interrogations" we'd called "cop mode" growing up, the rapid-fire barking of questions demanding an answer. Sitting in one of the chairs, I pulled him down in the other. "I'll tell you everything you want to know. Just sit."

He scooted his chair closer and turned, one hand coming up to curl along my jaw. From the corner of my eye I saw Remi tense, but he didn't interfere. "Just tell me you're okay. That's the most important thing."

Was I okay? Physically, yes, but emotionally I felt like I'd been through a war. "I'm okay."

His shoulders slumped, relief softening his face. And because I wanted that relief to stay, because I didn't want him on his knees again, I didn't explain immediately that Ross wasn't.

"Who are these men?"

Telling him the truth about the Agozis could put them in danger. "They're friends." I glanced Remi's way. "Remi is—"

"She's mine," Remi said when I faltered. An automatic denial rose to my lips, but I clamped them shut over it. I was his. What that meant for the future, I had no idea, but it didn't matter right now.

"Leah—"

My raised hand cut Dad off. "That's not important right now."

"Then what is?" He grabbed my hand from the air, gripping it tight. "Leah, what's going on? What happened to you?"

"I fell in love," I finally said.

"With him?" Dad jerked his chin toward Remi.

"No, not back then." Remi's intensity burned into my skin, and I knew he'd noticed how I avoided saying I didn't love him. "Seven years ago...I fell in love with a man named Angelo di Cosimo."

My father's eyes went round, fear making them wild. A curse left his lips.

"You knew him?" I asked.

"No," he bit out. "I didn't know him, but I remember the case. A known Fiori associate." His dark eyes narrowed on me. "How did you get involved with someone like that?"

So I told him the story, dragging up bits of my memories that I'd tried to forget, until I came to the night of Angelo's death.

"Why didn't you come to me, Leah? I would've taken care of you." Pain echoed through his voice, and guilt rose, threatening to choke me.

"Because..." I closed my eyes, wishing I could do anything but speak the next words that had to come out of my mouth. "Because I went to Ross first."

Dad jerked back. "What?" He shook his head. "Then why am I just hearing about this now and not seven years ago?"

"Dad... I..."

"Mr. Windon," Remi said, coming to my rescue, "your son was working with the Fioris."

"What? No!"

I squeezed Dad's hand tight. "Yes." Tears stung my eyes, and I couldn't hide them when Dad's gaze fixed on mine. "Yes, he was."

"He wanted the evidence," Remi added, "and Leah didn't have it, so she ran."

"Why? Why run?" Dad stood to pace, just like I did when I was frustrated. "I was right there at home waiting for you. You could've come to me at any time. Even if Ross—" He shook his head. "Even if he was working for the Fioris, I wouldn't have let them hurt you."

"Dad, I couldn't." How did I make him understand? "I wouldn't pit you against your own son." He would've had to choose, because one of us would be hurt—either me or Ross. The Fioris wouldn't have accepted failure.

"So you'd rather I lose my daughter?"

"No," I said quietly. "I'd rather I didn't lose mine."

Dad jerked to a stop, a stunned look spreading over his face. "You...you have a daughter?"

I nodded. "I was pregnant when I ran. Brooke was born six months later."

"Brooke." Dad wobbled his way back to his chair. I didn't blame him for being unsteady; at this point I was surprised I hadn't passed out. But I couldn't; the worst was yet to come.

And I couldn't be the one to reveal it to him. I just... I loved Ross; I couldn't bear to say the words I knew would make his death a reality not just for me, but for my father. My gaze sought Remi out, my lifeline, my partner.

He nodded, his beautiful amber eyes gleaming, telling me without words that he got the message.

"Ross..." Remi cleared his throat, the sound softening something buried beneath all the pain in my heart. Remi didn't want to say the words any more than I did; if he had, he'd have blurted it out for hardest effect. Instead he stumbled much like I had. "Sir, Ross was killed two days ago."

"No!"

The word hissed out of my father like a balloon losing air. I leaned into his side, laying my head on his shoulder like I had so many times as a child. His familiar lime and musk scent enveloped me as the tears began again. "It's true," I croaked. "It's true. He's gone."

Dad's arm came around me, gathering me close, comforting me when I should be the one comforting him. I could literally feel him gathering himself, feel his emotions slide away, leaving behind the cop he'd been all my life. The warrior. And I envied him in that moment.

"Who was it?" he asked.

Remi answered. "It was Fiori's men. And if you don't help us, they're going to keep trying to kill your daughter and granddaughter until they succeed."

Chapter Twenty-Six

Leah—

"I'm still not happy about this."

I glanced at Remi in the dark of the SUV's back seat. Levi had volunteered to drive my father to our hotel, separate from us. Maybe to have a little talk with him. Levi could scare the piss out of any man—and was probably attempting to do that with Dad at this very moment—but I'd been through the ringer tonight and couldn't bring myself to worry about it. If it made the brothers feel more secure, my dad could take it.

Remi didn't seem to be as accepting. Or maybe it was that he couldn't do it himself. But he'd already been away from me once tonight, and when the time had come to split up again, he'd kept me hard against him. Eli's teasing once we'd settled into the SUV had been met with a "fuck you" as Remi buckled me into the middle seat, right up against him, then curled my body close.

The protectiveness should be driving me nuts, but instead it was just another safety line holding me up. Or nail in my coffin, maybe. A rope tying me tighter to this man I'd never have dreamed I could love. The metaphors could go on, but they didn't really matter. What did was the fact that Remi didn't trust our safety to anyone easily. He cared for me. And for my child.

I breathed his scent deep into my lungs. Feeling hated tears pricking at the backs of my eyes again, I cuddled closer, seeking the comfort I knew he'd give without question. He picked up my legs, pulling them over his, and wrapped both arms around me, a wall between me and the world.

At the hotel we waited in the parking garage until the town car Levi was driving arrived. My dad got out of the back, and my chest ached at seeing the fatigue in his face, the slump of his shoulders and dragging of his feet. He had no one to comfort him but me. When the two men drew close, I reached for him. "Dad."

His big hand cupped my cheek as he leaned in, planting a kiss on my forehead just like he had so many times before. God, how I'd missed that simple gesture. The security of it, back when things had been simple and a father's kiss could cure anything. I sniffled.

Damn tears.

The elevator doors opened. Remi ushered us inside, but it wasn't until the doors closed that Dad spoke. "Where is Ross now?"

I closed my eyes. *Keep it together, Leah.* So much had happened that I wished my dad didn't have to know, but there was really no choice.

"He..." I opened my eyes, cleared my throat. "He and one of Fiori's henchman kidnapped Brooke. They wanted the recordings, but at the time we didn't know we had them."

Dad rubbed a hand over his face, leaving it over his mouth as he stared up at the display showing the floor numbers. Sixteen. Seventeen. Eighteen. He was shaking his head by nineteen, and I had to look away from the devastation so clear on his face.

Remi took over. "During our meet up to retrieve Brooke, Ross was shot by Joe Southerland—you may be familiar with him. Your son bled out before we could get him help."

"And is his body still there?" Dad asked, the words scratchy.

"He is," Levi said matter-of-factly, "along with Southerland and the associates he brought with him. Unfortunately the warehouse burned down, so it may be some weeks before you can claim the body."

The elevator stopped; the doors slid open. Dad exited blindly, holding up a hand when Remi directed him down the hall. "Just a moment."

He turned in the opposite direction, toward a window at the end of the hall. Remi and his brothers stayed with me, giving him space.

"We'll take him to the second suite," Remi said, his voice low. Levi and Eli both nodded.

I shook my head. "No."

"Leah—"

"Remi, no." Stepping close, I put my hand on his broad chest, willing him to understand what I was about to say. "He needs to see Brooke. After that, we can go wherever you want, but he needs to see her."

The muscles under my hand went rock-hard. "She's asleep; he won't get to meet her, just see her face. I don't like him knowing where we are."

I understood that, but... "He needs this. And more importantly, I need it. After he leaves, we can move her if you think it's safer, but he's going to see her tonight."

We stood for a long moment, and I knew his brothers were simply waiting on Remi's word. Whatever it was, they would carry it out, whether I agreed or not. Finally, reluctantly, Remi nodded. I pulled his head down for a kiss.

"Thank you," I said, just for him.

"Thank him later," Eli butted in. "We've got work to do."

I stuck my tongue out at the youngest Agozi brother just as my father rejoined us.

Taking Dad's hand, I led him down the hall to our suite. After knocking on the door—two soft, two hard, then two soft—Remi opened it and allowed us inside. Dain and King looked up from different points of the room, and I could see from the widening of their eyes the moment our guest's identity registered. No one made introductions. The brothers piled in as I led my father to the bedroom door and turned the knob.

We tiptoed inside.

Light filtered in from the cracked bathroom door, illuminating Abby where she sat in a chair at Brooke's bedside. Seeing us, she stood, moving silently back to allow us close. My dad's fingers tightened on mine, the realization of what we were doing hitting him, I guess. It was hitting me too, but I couldn't tell if it was excitement or terror stirring up trouble in my stomach. I tugged him toward the head of the bed, where Brooke's face peeked out from a cocoon of blankets and pillows.

A choked sound, quickly smothered, left Dad's lips. He went to his knees for the second time tonight.

I knelt beside him. "She's been through a lot," I said, hoping he'd understand why I didn't wake her.

A shaky hand reached out, faltered, then fell to the blanket, careful not to wake Brooke. "She looks just like you," he whispered hoarsely. "Just like your mother." His breath hitched in his throat. "So grown-up. I've missed so much."

Because of me, my decisions. "I'm sorry. I don't know if you can ever forgive me—"

"Stop that." Fierce eyes that matched my own turned to me. "This wasn't your fault."

"It is. Ross..." I struggled to hold back tears. "Ross is dead because of me."

"No, he isn't." He reached for me then, hand wrapped around my neck, thumb stroking my jaw. "If what your friend said was true, Ross made his choices."

His disappointment stabbed at me. "I'm not so sure he did, Dad. The initial one, maybe. But I don't think he would ever have taken Brooke of his own accord."

Glancing over his shoulder, my dad asked, "Are you sure they"—he jerked his head toward the door, where Remi waited on the other side—"can be trusted? Really trusted, Leah? What if they made up the story about Ross?"

I hated to tear apart his hope, but... "It's the truth, Dad. I was there; I saw what happened."

As if his very soul deflated, my dad slumped against the bed. He glanced at Brooke again. "Did they hurt her?"

"No." Finally something positive I could share. "Ross protected her as much as possible."

He nodded, his thumb still absently stroking my face, his gaze centered on Brooke. "That man out there, the one who's claimed you—"

"Remi." Not his full name, hopefully not enough to identify him if anything went wrong, but I wanted my father to have some sort of human connection to the man I loved.

"Remi." His tone wasn't any warmer than before he'd known Remi's name. "He's a killer, Leah. You can see it in his eyes."

When he looked at anyone but me, yes. "You can't tell the full extent of a man's character just from his eyes."

"I've seen plenty of killers; trust me, it's there." He sighed, staring back at Brooke. "Of course, I never saw betrayal in my own son's eyes."

Neither did I. "I know Remi, Dad. I—" *Love him.* But I couldn't say it, not yet. Remi should be the first to hear those words from me.

Dad turned to me, his gaze full of fire. "Would you bet your life on him? Brooke's life?"

"I would." No hesitation. "I already have."

He stared down at me for the longest moment. Finally, he pushed to his feet. "All right. Let's see if he's got a good enough plan to get this mess untangled, then. Come on."

In the living room, only Remi and his brothers remained. Gesturing to the couch, Remi urged us to sit. "Need anything, *lev sheli?*"

My dad quirked a brow at the phrase but didn't ask questions. Remi scrounged up a soda I hoped would settle my stomach, then brought Dad a coffee before settling on the arm of the chair across from us. Levi took one end of the seating area, Eli the other.

Dad eyed the arrangement as he took a sip of his coffee. "Leah said earlier you didn't know you had the recordings when you went to meet Ross and Southerland. I take it you have them now."

"We found them in a necklace Angelo gave Leah," Remi confirmed.

"And what do you plan to do with them?"

Remi cocked his head, the predator rising in his eyes. "That depends on you."

Chapter Twenty-Seven

Remi—

Ross Windon Sr agreed to stay with us. Saved me the hassle of forcing him to. That would've put a serious damper on any future relationship we might have, and I didn't need him interfering with Leah for the rest of our lives. Seeing me follow Leah into the bedroom to sleep near Brooke already had a sour look crossing his face. I'd let Levi do any further antagonizing that became necessary.

Leah stood at the foot of the bed, staring at the tiny bump of Brooke's body beneath a mound of covers. The rigid set to her spine and the tense grip she had on her elbows shouted her anger more clearly than any words. Not at me, I didn't think, or anyone else here. At the circumstances. The situation she found herself and her daughter in. The absolute, complete and utter unfairness of it all.

And we'd just added insult to injury.

"Leah..."

She glanced my way without meeting my eyes, but I could see the glistening of tears in hers. "Santo Fiori should be punished."

I moved behind her, circled her body with my arms, wishing they were strong enough to hold every bad thing at bay.

"For the things he's done to others," she continued, "but not just that. I want him dead, Remi.

I want it so much I feel like I'll choke on it. For the things he's done to my daughter, to me. I want him tortured and scarred; I want him to lose everything he's ever cherished, and then I want him dead."

I tucked my head down until my nose met her hair, breathed in that scent that was uniquely Leah's. "I know."

Her hands came up to grip my arms. "This won't really be a punishment, will it?"

No, because the head of the Fiori mob family would live. The Fioris would continue with crime as usual, and the people Leah loved would be no more than a small glitch in their day. Life wasn't fair. Leah knew that better than anyone—she'd lost so much of her life because of this man, this family. I wanted justice for the things that had been done to her too, but we couldn't risk a war with the mob, not if we wanted to guarantee Leah's and Brooke's freedom. This plan would protect her, but the cost of that protection was tearing her apart.

There was only one thing I could give her.

Bending closer to her ear, I spoke softly. "Men like Fiori always get what's coming to them in the end."

"Do they?"

She didn't believe it right now, but eventually she would. When it was safe.

"They do."

Adjusting my hold, I ducked lower, pushing aside the long strands of blonde hair until soft, sensitive skin was revealed. My lips came to rest right beneath her ear where the scent of her, the heat of her was strongest. "It may not be tomorrow, or the day after, or the next after that." We were too close; anything that happened to Fiori could be too easily tied to the woman I held safely in my arms. "But eventually justice comes for every one of the bastards like Fiori. It will come for him too."

Leah's breath stilled; her heartbeat picked up beneath my lips. "Does justice have a name?"

"Doesn't need one." I nipped at her skin, drawing a gasp, forcing her to breathe. "As long as it comes, the name doesn't matter."

She tipped her head to the side, giving me greater access. "How do you do that, Remi?"

"Jeremiah," I growled into her shoulder.

"Jeremiah," she breathed, and shivered against me. "Don't get me wrong; if I had the chance, I'd kill Fiori in a heartbeat. But my hatred for the Fioris, that's personal. How...how do you decide, every day, who lives or dies, and still sleep at night?"

There was no judgment in the question, not even curiosity, really. Just a need to know. I wasn't sure I could explain. Maybe the piece of me that shied away from killing had been missing from birth. Maybe it had been torn away when my parents were murdered, when I'd walked into their bedroom and stepped on that blood-spattered carpet. Maybe the years of scrambling to survive in a world whose sole aim was to eat us alive had done the damage. I didn't know, and honestly, at this point in my life, I didn't care.

"You're a nurse," I finally said. "Your job is to treat the sick, no matter who it is. My job, until now, has been to serve justice however it needs to be served. Maybe it doesn't keep me awake at night because I'm no random killer; every job has a purpose. We have one rule: Don't harm the innocent. Fiori hasn't been innocent in a long, long time. If anything happens to him in the future as a result of his own actions"—I shrugged—"I'm good with that."

I waited, knowing she got my point, knowing she understood that, though the immediate outcome of Brooke's kidnapping would not be satisfactory, Fiori's punishment was only being delayed. I'd take care of it.

Long moments later, her body relaxed back against mine. "As long as Brooke is safe," she said quietly.

I pressed my palm over her stomach, melding her body to mine. "As long as you're both safe."

My heart jumped when her hands came back to cup my ass, pull me closer. "You said 'until now.' What does that mean?"

Far too much for me to explain at the foot of her sleeping daughter's bed at one in the morning. "We can work on that when this is all over, *lev sheli.*"

She hummed, whether in agreement or because of the endearment or because I was tracing biting kisses down her neck, I wasn't sure. The next moment she stepped out of my arms. "Take a shower with me?"

My dick punched at my zipper. It was the first time Leah had initiated contact of any kind between us, the first time she'd signaled that she wanted me without me approaching her first. I threw a look to where Brooke slept soundly, then took Leah's hand. "Hell yeah." Always.

In the bathroom, I moved to the shower and turned the water on to warm. Facing her felt like coming home, and I found myself wanting to slow down time, to savor the moment instead of rushing forward. Maybe she did too, because she didn't hurry to undress. Instead her eyes held mine as I grasped the hem of my shirt and pulled it over my head, tossed it into the corner.

Leah leaned her hip against the counter.

My fingers went to the button of my fatigues. "I thought this was a joint thing."

A faint smile pulled at her lips despite the fatigue darkening the skin beneath her eyes, slumping over her shoulders. "Just looking. Maybe I don't get enough chances to just look."

Considering the frenzy we'd been in each time we came together, she had a point. I flicked my pants open, eased the zipper down. Women had admired my body since I'd begun filling out as a teen, but the heat flaring in Leah's eyes, the hunger that licked over my skin everywhere her gaze touched—I'd never experienced anything like it. This woman touched my heart as well as my body. She ignited a need inside me that threatened to explode, and all she'd done was stare.

I snagged a condom from a pocket of my pants before sliding them down my legs. Kicked off my shoes, then the fatigues, not caring where they landed. All I cared about was the slide of Leah's tongue across her lips as her gaze landed on my rock-hard cock.

"Your turn," I said, prowling forward.

She watched me slide the condom on, her arms tightening over her middle, plumping her breasts up so that they flirted with the low vee of her T-shirt. I dropped my gaze to the rounded flesh as I planted my fists on either side of her hips and leaned down. Only her hand on my chest stopped me, stroking over the scar from the gunshot wound that had landed me in the hospital. The injury that had brought us together eighteen months ago.

I'd almost died. And I'd found my life, in this woman, this moment.

Leah's gasping breath filled my ears, her taste filling my mouth when I opened my lips over the luscious curve of her breast and sucked.

"Jeremiah."

The word was rough, breathless. It sent a jolt of hunger through my gut. I needed more—more flesh, more desire, more of Leah. A whole lot more.

With a yank I stretched the neck of her tee down until it cupped her breast. A ripping sound reached my ears, but I ignored it, ignored everything but the mound pushed toward my mouth as I dragged her bra down too. A ripe pink nipple reached for me. I took the crinkled length between my lips and drew on it, forced it against the roof of my mouth and sucked hard.

Not enough. It was never enough with Leah, but now, here, I wanted everything she had to give. Fuck patience and savoring. That first taste of her had torn through any control I'd thought I had. Taking the neck of her shirt in both fists, I ripped it straight down the middle as I continued to suck.

Leah arched against me. "Yes. God yes."

Luckily for her lingerie, the bra had a front clasp that opened when I fumbled with it. Finesse was beyond me—I needed access, and when the cloth gave, I brought both hands to her breasts, pushed them together, took turns with her nipples. Teeth, tongue, lips. I devoured her, only vaguely aware of the cries she muffled behind her hand as I took what I so desperately needed.

"Remi, please!"

Without warning Leah pulled away from me. I felt the cool counter kiss my erection and realized she'd raised herself on top of it. Taking advantage, I ripped open her jeans and stripped the rest of her clothes off.

Then tipped her back against the mirror, raised her feet to the counter, and set about devouring her in a whole different way.

Slender fingers dug into my hair, pulling my head close. Leah's clit was a hard button peeking from between deep pink lips. I grasped it gently with my teeth, giving her the suction she needed, the pressure that had her pelvis rocking against my face, her fingers digging deep, her strangled cries escaping despite her best efforts. "That's it, *lev sheli*," I said, raising my head just long enough to slip my fingers into her cream-covered slit. "That's it. Use me good. Get off on me."

She cocked her hips, and my fingers slid deeper. I curled them against her G-spot, took that sensitive nub back into my mouth. Leah rode my hand hard, and my heart and cock throbbed in unison at her taste, the feel of her, the knowledge that I was the one giving her this pleasure. My woman. My heart. She was my everything.

"Remi, it's coming," she whispered roughly above my head. I pressed my fingers deep, rubbing against that soft pad deep inside her. Leah whined as the first contraction squeezed around my invasion.

I needed to feel it on my cock, not just my fingers. Sliding out, I pulled her hips to the edge of the counter and slid my thick, hard length inside. A cry escaped her as I crowded in, taking up every millimeter of space and forcing her to squeeze down on something far thicker than my fingers. I eased back, then surged forward, even deeper this time, and held myself there as her orgasm threatened to squeeze the life out of me.

"Fuck, Leah," I whispered in her ear. "You're so tight, so strong. Squeeze me, *lev sheli*. You're gonna suck me dry, aren't you?"

"God, I want to," she said, the words strained. A quiver shot through her. "I want you."

The clenching around my cock eased to flutters. I pulled back, pushed deep, setting up a rhythm. I should stop, give her time. But the feel of Leah's wet flesh cupping me, clutching me...fuck if I could find the strength to force myself away.

I threw my head back, a groan escaping. "I need you so fucking much, *lev sheli*."

Leah tightened around me. "What does it mean, Jeremiah?" Delicate fingers traced across my chest. Pinched my tight nipples, drawing as hard a gasp from me as I'd drawn from her earlier. "What's *lev sheli*?"

"Leah." Ah God. I couldn't stop. The glide of her up and down my cock, the feel of her cream dripping down to coat my balls... "Leah!"

"Tell me." Leaving my nipples behind, her fingers glided down my abs, making them clench, ripple with pleasure. Short fingernails traced the trail of hair from my navel to my cock. When she wrapped her fingers around the solid bar of my shaft, I went to my toes, pushing as high and hard inside her as I could. "Tell me what it means."

My eyes were crossing. I blinked back the need consuming me and focused on her face, on the look in her eyes. Heavy-lidded, her gaze was full of a hunger that matched my own, but that wasn't all. There was something else staring back at me, something I hardly dared believe: acceptance. Leah was fucking a killer, and looked at me like that.

God help me.

The slap of skin against skin filled the room as my hips sped up without permission, reaching, desperate for that melding I only wanted with her. That I needed so desperately I thought I'd go insane.

"What does it mean, Jeremiah?"

I more saw than heard the question, watched her lips wrap around my name. "My heart," I gasped, lunging again and again. "My heart, Leah."

A Cleopatra smile curved her lips. The fingers around my cock retreated, and as I looked down, I saw her press hard on her clit. She shifted her weight onto her feet, swinging her hips into each advance. Once. Twice.

My balls drew up. A tingle shot from my head to the base of my spine, and I knew I was done for.

"Leah!" I laid myself down on her, using my weight to force myself inside. "Leah!"

She clenched herself around me, that smile still on her lips. "You're my heart too, Jeremiah."

I let go then, releasing inside her. Making her mine. And when Leah's climax hit just behind mine, I knew I belonged to her as well. For however long she'd have me.

Chapter Twenty-Eight

Remi—

The Fiori family was patriarchal, as were most mob families. Every decision, every deal was run through Santo "Sonny" Fiori, the grandfather of the family. But as I watched the man on the screen in front of me fuck the woman in his bed, I couldn't help thinking how natural a heart attack would be at that age, especially for a man with Fiori's appetites. Filing the idea away, I checked my weapons once more before turning to Levi.

"This might take a while."

"Not likely," Eli said from the back seat. "The man's too old to hold out long with a woman like that."

Considering she was a good sixty years his junior, Eli wasn't wrong. And the likelihood that she was there willingly wasn't high.

We waited impatiently for the man's final rough grunts. I grimaced, disgusted, as he rolled off the woman's body a few moments later, his wet penis flopping against his thigh. The way the woman curled away from him confirmed my earlier thoughts. Nothing we could do about it tonight, but later, we could give her options to get out.

"You have the recording?" I asked Eli.

"I'm not a total fuckup, you know."

"Could've fooled me," Levi said, his face tight with concentration. We were like the three bears on an op—Levi dead serious, Eli joking to relieve the tension, and me somewhere in between. Just right, as I liked to refer to it. When we left the safety of the SUV, it would be a different story, but right now...

It took only a few minutes for Fiori to fall asleep, still splayed like an upended frog across the bed. The woman took longer. A half hour after she drifted off, we moved out. The rain had started earlier, but as we neared Fiori's property, lightning flashed across the sky, followed by the crash of thunder.

"Handy," Eli said, his voice reaching me in the mic I'd tucked into my ear. "Dogs will be going crazy."

I acknowledged the gift with a grunt and proceeded along the back fence of the five-acre property Fiori occupied when he was in town. Modest compared to the Italian villa on the coast of Sicily or his Maui estate, but convenient. And easier to police, this close to his family's enemies.

They hadn't seen an enemy like us, though.

With the storm, patrols had dwindled to one every ten minutes or so. We waited for the latest guard, the accompanying German shepherd hesitating at the end of his leash for no more than a moment before being led forward with a rough command. Eli had already hacked Fiori's security. Now the mini computer strapped to his forearm allowed him to flicker the power once, twice, before cutting it just long enough for us to climb the electrified fence.

"Good thing they don't have a backup generator." I carefully straddled the discreet but definitely there barbed wire atop the barrier.

"Oh, they do."

My balls did a rapid retreat into my body. "What?" I hissed at my brother. A sloppy scramble got me over the side for a quick jump to the ground.

Eli's laugh was quiet in my ear, but the lack of volume couldn't hide his sadistic amusement. "I said they had a backup; I didn't say it was useable. Unfortunately for them, it's experiencing technical difficulties."

"Are we doing this, or are we hanging here for a chat?" Levi muttered.

Eli dropped to the ground between us. "Just a sec."

Electricity hummed along the fence, barely audible. Lights dulled by the storm flickered back on.

Crouching, the three of us ran for the nearby woods. Unlike our estate, Fiori had left the land surrounding his mansion wild. Looked pretty, but it was shit for security. We were within a hundred yards of the house in less than five minutes, without even a close call.

"Thank fuck for waterproof gear," Eli said in my earpiece.

No kidding.

Crouching in the underbrush, we gave Eli a few minutes to flicker the power a couple more times, allowing security to lower their guard where the electricity was concerned. When Levi gave the signal, Eli sent the command to his keypad and the lights went out.

Levi shot from cover immediately. I was directly on his heels, Eli just behind. Levi had a grappling hook secured to the roof in seconds. No more than four minutes passed before the three of us were inside the obscenely large bathroom attached to Fiori's master suite.

Eli turned the power back on.

"Get the alarm taken care of," Levi warned. Even without the backup generator, the alarm system had its own battery pack. It would've registered the window opening. Too bad the system included a connection to the Internet in order to send information back and forth to the off-site security company. Easy access for them—and for us.

"On it."

Levi moved to the bathroom door. I opened a side pocket on my fatigues and pulled out the prepped needle waiting there. We couldn't remove the woman, not without making her a target— disappearing might give the impression that she'd helped us—but we could keep her from knowing what was going on. Levi signaled with four fingers, counting down. Four… Three… Two… At one he opened the door, allowing me to slip past.

The girl was taken care of without trouble. The needle slipped into her arm without waking her, the effect of the ketamine almost immediate. We gave it several more minutes before my brothers made quick work of gagging and securing Fiori to his own bed— as roughly as possible.

I watched. Waited. Let the killer slip to the fore.

Finally Fiori was settled against the headboard— or maybe I should say trussed to it. Levi did enjoy his ropes; they meant his victims could be fully awake for their torture. I moved to the end of the bed, feet braced apart, arms crossed over my chest.

"Good evening, Sonny," I said.

Fiori huffed angrily behind his gag. A few moments of mumbling followed.

"I imagine you're asking about your guards. Or warning me that they'll catch us." I gave him a small, grim smile. "Unfortunately for you, we know your suite is soundproof, for obvious reasons." I glanced at the woman, sleeping peacefully on her side, facing away from Fiori. "They'll find you, of course. When we're ready."

Fiori growled, anger shining from his beady eyes.

"Relax, Gramps." I stared into those eyes, letting him see exactly how little his anger affected me. How I didn't give a fuck if he was comfortable, if he thought he could buy his way out of this, if he swore retaliation the minute he was free. None of it mattered. He couldn't touch me; he'd learn that soon enough.

"We are here about a little matter that may have come to your attention: Leah Windon?"

Fiori's eyes rounded before narrowing, his face turning an interesting shade of red detectable even in the dim light of the room.

"You sent a team to recover certain"— deliberately I glanced at Levi as if considering— "evidence. Yes?"

The man on the bed jerked at his bonds, glaring at me.

"Exactly." Reaching into the sheath at the small of my back, I drew my KA-BAR, held it in front of me. "I see you remember."

Fiori zeroed in on the knife in my hand.

"You see…" I moved around the end of the bed, noting the cord securing Fiori's legs in front of him, the bare feet so vulnerable to anything I needed to do.

"Leah is under our protection." The knife's tip glinted wickedly as I lowered it to stroke the top of the nearest foot. "And we don't like it when anyone steps into our business. *Anyone*, Sonny."

A flick, and the first slice appeared just below his toes—long, shallow, barely enough to bleed. It stung, I knew, sent a shock through the man's system, but that was nothing more than foreplay.

Fiori jerked. A single word, barked behind his gag, came through clearly.

"Who? Is that what you asked?" Fiori whined as I moved the knife to his other foot, took my sample cut from the hair-covered knob of his big toe this time. "That's not really important, is it? Who we are will never matter if you stop pursuing what is mine. If you choose to ignore my warning"—I moved the knife to hover above foot number one, shrugged— "who we are will be equally unimportant. Because you'll be dead."

Another slice, deeper this time. Blood trickled toward the sheets. A warning growl came from behind Fiori's gag.

"That is definitely not the response I was looking for." A second cut on foot number two. "Careful, Sonny boy. Your balls are next."

Instinctively the man's thighs squeezed together. Ignoring the satisfaction his fear gave me, I motioned Eli forward. "You might be wondering what's in this deal for you besides staying alive." Eli held up the hand with the computer attached, pushed a couple of buttons. "Maybe this will help."

Fiori's voice fill the room. "Vincenzo is an idiot. If he'd wanted to stay alive, he'd never have crossed me. Those cement shoes were earned, a hundred percent."

Eli stopped the recording. I kept my gaze on Fiori. "Not too incriminating, is it? How about another one?"

Eli pressed the button. "What, you think Frankie has a fucking chance in hell of taking over my routes? No one, and I do mean *no one*, will be horning in on the drug supply in this town. I control every step, every participant, from the cooks to the candymen on the street to the importers and most especially the exports." Fiori boasted about his drug lines and how easy it was to control the penny-ante dealers who cluttered the DC streets. Trying to impress someone he wanted to do business with, most likely. Unfortunately he spilled a few too many details. Judging by the increasing struggles against his bonds and the alarming shade of purple creeping into his face, I was pretty sure he knew that.

"I like that one," I said, smirking, when Eli stopped the tape again. Dragging the tip of my knife along the ridge of Fiori's shinbone, over his knee, and up his thigh, I said, "Angelo di Cosimo was good at finding incriminating evidence, wasn't he? He knew exactly where to hit, what to search for. When to record it. That's not my favorite, though. This one is."

"I want Windon dead," Fiori said on the recording. "Do you hear me? You think I can't touch your old man? How do you think he got the fucking job? The previous commissioner got a little too close to things he shouldn't be close to. I took him out, and I can take your father out too, Junior. Give me a reason not to."

Fiori's legs trembled as I flipped the sheet off his naked lap. My knife tip dug into the crease between his thigh and flaccid, still-sticky penis. "Ross Windon Jr agreed to work for you to keep his family safe. He even, after all these years, agreed to kidnap his niece, knowing it was the only way he could keep her safe from you." I flicked the knife, and a shallow slice appeared along the side of Fiori's dick. "He's dead, you know. So are your men. Want to know who killed them?"

The mobster held himself rigid, but he couldn't control his flinch as the knife kissed his dick again. A panicked cry escaped around his gag.

"You want to know, don't you?" I added a third cut, the high whine I received in response satisfying something primal, something dominant deep inside me. The animal beneath my veneer of civilization ate up the man's fear like it was fucking prime rib. "That was us, Sonny." Flick. "The men who killed your team." Flick. "The men with the recordings you were after." Flick. "The men who wouldn't even flinch if we thought killing you would stop all this."

"Castration sounds good to me," Levi said from the dark. Fiori jerked, then cried out when the knife bit into his thigh.

I tsked. "Need to be careful there." Wiping the blood from my blade on the man's leg, I narrowed my gaze on him. "You have a choice. Only one."

A bushy brow rose over one eye. I didn't miss the strain it took to respond so nonchalantly. It was evident in the sweat popping up on Fiori's forehead.

"You can walk away from the Windon family— not for a little while. Permanently. Walk away and it will be like none of this ever happened."

A grunt from Fiori.

"Or…" I gestured toward Eli with the KA-BAR. "Or these recordings are going public. Not just to the commissioner—that would be far too easy to erase. No, we have copies set to deliver to every reporter in the DC area, every cop, every DA. You name them and they're on our list. Isn't the electronic age fun?"

Leah's father had the original chip, hidden in a secret safe deposit box, but Eli had already set up a mass e-mail list with copies.

I leaned closer. "Of course, you would be facing those charges alone, since every member of your family would be dead before you could blink. Don't think we could do it?" I shook my head. "Neither did your team in Atlanta. Or your security here. Think about that."

Fiori's eyes closed tight. I should've been pleased with the frustration on his face, the realization that he was out of options. I wasn't. I wanted to kill the fucker, but Levi was right—the mob was a hydra; cut off one head and three more popped up. No, the only way to keep Fiori from retaliating against Leah's family was to hold something over his head.

When this night was a distant memory? That's when I would get what I truly wanted, when it could no longer be tied to Leah.

"So what do you say, Sonny?" I nodded toward the woman in his bed. "Want to keep up your whoring and drug dealing and money laundering and, I don't know, *living*? Or should we take care of this now?" I brought the knife to his fat neck and waited.

Fiori pressed himself back into the headboard, shaking his head vigorously.

"No?" I wagged the knife at him. "Is that no deal, no, you don't want to keep living?" The tip of the KA-BAR tapped the man's cheek. "Or no, don't kill me here and now, before we slit your throat?"

"Don't forget the castrating," Levi threw in.

"Who would want to forget that?" I cocked a brow at our captive. "What's your answer?"

Fiori dipped his eyes down, indicating the gag. Sliding the knife under the cloth where it lay on his cheek, I tugged. The knife cut through the gag like it was butter.

Fiori choked. "Don't hurt me. Don't."

"So we have a deal?"

He nodded jerkily, eyes on the knife. "We have a deal."

Chapter Twenty-Nine

Leah—

Dad had turned the scraps of a napkin from the coffee supplies into a match game. Brooke was currently studying the blank squares, tongue peeking from between her lips, trying to determine which scrap to turn over to match the star she'd already found. My father's gaze was riveted on her. Was he remembering all the times we'd sat around the kitchen table after dinner and played games just like that? Half of our family was gone now, half of the people who'd sat around that table and shared their lives, their joy. Watching my family now, I felt my chest go tight and tears prick the backs of my eyes.

"She's really taken to him," Elliot said, coming up beside me. The team didn't know everything about my past, but they did know my dad had met Brooke for the first time only a couple of days ago.

"She has." I glanced to the far end of the suite where King, Saint, and Dain were packing up the team's equipment. "I can't thank you all enough for keeping her safe for me."

Elliot grinned. "For me, with Sydney at home, this was a tame assignment. For them"—she gestured to the men—"it was good practice. Dain's baby will be here in, like, six weeks. He needed some kid exposure. The other two needed practice babysitting."

I hadn't realized Dain's wife was pregnant. As the team lead and the oldest of the four, I'd have figured he was past the baby-making stage, but then again, the man's dark, sexy eyes had the kind of intensity that could probably impregnate a woman from fifty yards away, so...

Remi was twenty-nine, he'd said. How did he feel about having kids in his thirties or forties? How did I feel?

Was I really thinking about having more kids, with an assassin?

A hand sneaked around my waist, making me jump. Remi. I knew the second his warmth hit me, his scent filled my nose. I'd been too involved in my thoughts to notice his approach. I'd love to blame my lack of sleep last night, but no—I'd been that enthralled with thoughts of babies and Remi whirling in my head.

"Okay?" he asked.

Of course he didn't look preoccupied. Or tired. He'd slept in the armchair in the corner of the bedroom for the early part of the evening last night, but I had awakened after midnight to the closing of our door. Knowing where he was going, I hadn't been able to fall back to sleep until hours later when he'd snuck back in. He'd been dozing in the chair when Brooke got up at the crack of dawn. Without blinking he'd urged her into the living area, telling me to close my eyes again, but my efforts to do just that had been fruitless. There was too much I didn't know, too much uncertainty going forward for me to relax.

Which meant I probably looked like death warmed over right now, unlike Mr. Capable.

"I'm fine."

Remi opened his mouth, but Dain's arrival forestalled any response he could make. Probably a good thing.

Dain indicated their equipment. "We're ready to head out when you are. Saint has confirmed the plane is on the tarmac, prepped and waiting. Just say the word."

Remi nodded. "We'll be ready in a few minutes if you'd like to go ahead and start loading up." He reached out a hand. "If I forget to tell you later, thank you."

Dain shook. "Of course. If you need us in the future, you know where to find us."

Dain had to have some idea of what the brothers were, that everything here had not been on the up-and-up. Surely Charlotte knew something, had told King. Maybe it was easy for them to compartmentalize, to focus on their part of the job— keeping Brooke and me safe—and ignore everything else, but meeting Dain's intense gaze, I knew he knew something. And yet he seemed totally at ease with the idea of working with the Agozis again.

Shouldn't that tell you something?

Dain and Elliot went to begin loading the equipment. Remi spared a glance for my dad playing with Brooke, then his brothers handling what little luggage we had, before tugging me into the bedroom. I followed willingly, though my throat went dry when he locked the door behind us.

"We need to talk."

I winced. Somehow I'd thought we'd do this when we got back to the mansion. That I'd have more time. That I wouldn't be so torn when it came down to the moment when Remi broached a conversation about our future. And that's what this was; I knew it. The threat of the Fioris was gone. Remi wasn't the type of man to just go with the flow and let the future take care of itself.

Deep breath, Leah. "Okay."

He sat on the edge of the bed. When I came close, he grabbed my hips in his big hands and pulled me where he wanted me, right between his legs. Heat flashed through my body.

"We'll be home soon," he said, the rough rumble of his voice doing nothing to ease the need inside me. We hadn't been alone since the night before last, the night he'd blown away any preconceived notions I'd had about how good the sex could be between us. I hadn't stopped craving him since.

It was his words that put a damper on my libido. I stared down at his chest like a coward. "I know."

His fingers dug into my flesh. "So…what's next? Where are you going when we get back?"

I reached for him then, my hands on his biceps anchoring me through the storm beginning to swirl in my head. "Remi—"

"Because I know exactly where I want you to go, *lev sheli.* I just don't think you're ready for that."

Lev sheli. My heart. My own heart melted every time he said it.

I forced myself to meet his shining amber eyes. "Are you saying you love me?"

Remi's chest expanded as he took a deep breath, his pecs brushing my nipples. "I don't love you, Leah."

My heart dropped to my feet.

"What I feel for you isn't anything as fragile as love." Reaching up, he gripped my jaw, his thumbs brushing my lips. "I thought that's what it was for the longest time, but not now. I'm not even sure there's a word powerful enough to describe what I feel for you. I can't breathe without you. I can't think. I can't bear to think about you not being with me; I think it might destroy me if we have to go back to living without you as a part of me. I need you, Leah. You're mine. I—"

Leaning in, I pressed my mouth to his, stealing whatever words he'd been about to say. No doubt they'd been beautiful, but I didn't need them. He'd shattered my heart already.

Remi was smiling when I drew back. He took in the tears dripping down my cheeks, and the smile vanished. "Hey…"

"No." I shook my head. "It's okay." Now it was my turn to cradle his face in my hands. "I love you," I choked out. "I'm not poetic and the words might seem inadequate, but I do." Stroking the stubble he hadn't bothered to shave this morning, I fought to say what I needed to say. "I love you, but I don't know how to do this. I have a child. I have to think of Brooke's safety first." As much as it was ripping me apart inside.

Remi pulled me down until I was sitting in his lap. "I would never put Brooke at risk."

"But this, what you do"—I waved a hand at the hotel room—"isn't that the same thing?"

Remi's forehead met mine. I watched his eyes slide closed, the frustration creasing his brow. I'd never want to tear him away from his brothers, to make him choose, but I couldn't deny that my breath had stopped and I was fiercely, frantically hoping that he would choose me. *Please please please choose me.*

When Remi took my kiss, his tongue tasted of a desperation of his own.

My heart was racing as he broke away. He eased me back, giving us both space, and dread tightened my chest.

"I don't have all the answers," he finally said. His eyes, when they met mine, had darkened to copper. "I don't know what to do. But I know one thing—I'll do whatever I have to, to keep you." His fingers dug into my hair and grabbed tight. "Can you accept that for now? Let us make these decisions together?"

Time. He was asking for time. But what if he decided he couldn't walk away from killing? What if he couldn't—

What if? What if? The questions were never going to end. Could I let go of having all the answers now? Because that's what I really needed to ask myself. If Remi decided to choose the life he led over the life we could have, would I regret taking what little time I might have left with him?

No, I wouldn't regret it. How could I regret taking a chance on the man who meant more to me than anyone in my life besides my daughter?

I gave myself one more moment, then… "I won't move Brooke right now. She needs the stability of her home, her life." Of course the state of that home might mean a delay, given the state it had been in when I left, but still… "I'm not going to uproot her, not until things are…definite." Until the questions were answered and I knew for sure, a hundred percent

Remi's body relaxed against me, relief softening the tension in his face. "No, of course not. We've got time."

My fingers clenched, scraping against his beard again. "Yes, we do. I love you, Remi."

"You own me, *lev sheli*," he said roughly. Using his grip on my hair, he pulled me down beside him as he lay back on the bed. "You've always owned me. You always will."

I hoped so. As Remi took my mouth again, I stared into his beautiful eyes and knew he owned me as well. The assassin I'd trusted with my heart.

Epilogue

Two months later

Remi—

I finally ran Levi to ground in the basement. There'd been a strain around him lately; since I'd made things official with Leah, actually. He'd always been the one in control, but now our family was changing. It was hard for any of us to accept, but especially for him.

And now it was about to change even more. Fiori was dead—heart attack, or so everyone believed; I couldn't help feeling a bit smug about that—and it was time for Leah and me to move on. Together.

"Hey, can we talk?" I asked, dropping down on the couch next to him. Levi paused his game without looking at me. Not a good sign.

I waited. He'd acknowledge me when he was ready, though the tension in his shoulders told me he really didn't want to.

Finally he threw his controller onto the little table in front of us. "When you leaving?"

Not the direction I was going, but... "In a few hours. Got a hot date with a six-year-old."

Levi turned to me then. "What the fuck are you talking about?"

My confusion got worse. "What the fuck are you talking about?"

"Are you moving?"

"What? When?"

Levi rubbed a hand down his face. "I assumed soon. Isn't that what you came to tell me?"

"Hell no."

Some of the tension in my brother's body eased. "So where are you going?"

"To Leah's, tonight. Brooke challenged me to a rematch since I beat her at Apples To Apples." It wasn't Cards Against Humanity by any means, but sometimes I could get Leah to play with me after Brooke went to bed, and those games were always dirty. Especially when I made up the matches.

"Oh." He picked his controller back up, fiddled with it, but I noticed the game stayed paused.

"I'm not moving, Levi, but I did want to talk to you about a move."

More fiddling. "You don't need my permission."

No, I didn't. But this was *our* home, not mine. And what I was proposing might mean big changes for all of us.

"I want to ask Leah to move in with me here."

As soon as the words left me, I lost the ability to breathe. This was only the first hurdle, but a big one. If Levi didn't want my woman and her daughter—especially her daughter—in our home, then I would be talking about me moving. I didn't want that. I loved my family, all of it. I wanted every member under one roof, not this constant scattered feeling, the gnawing knowledge that I could only protect Leah and Brooke part of the time.

"Leah moving in means Brooke comes with her. Having a child here…"

"Would be different."

At least he didn't say *difficult*. Or flat-out no.

"There's something else you should know."

Levi stood abruptly. An ache started up between my eyes.

"I've been discussing things with Branson." Our head of security at Hacr had been there since our uncle's death over a decade ago. He was a good man, but getting older. "He's asked to retire next year. I want to take his place."

Levi jerked to a stop between one pacing step and the next, spun to face me. "You're taking yourself out of the field?"

I stood too, needing to be on the same level as he was. My future was at stake here, mine and Leah's, and yet it felt far too much like I was abandoning the man who'd raised me. "Levi, I will always have your back. Yours and Eli's. Don't ever think anything else." I hesitated. "I need... I want a family with Leah. In a perfect world our lives would've been much different and there would be no question that I would marry her, have children, be...normal. But the three of us, we're not normal. After what she's been through, I can't ask her to accept the risk that having an *active* assassin as her husband would bring."

I rounded the couch to move closer to him. "I won't be in the field, but I also won't deny you if you need me. Which is another reason I want them here, not me somewhere else, where you might not be able to get to me. Our family belongs together."

Levi resumed his pacing, and I waited. In reality it didn't matter if we agreed or not. This house, like the company, had been divided equally between the three of us. But I wouldn't bring Leah and Brooke here if they were unwanted; they didn't deserve that.

"You're planning to marry her?" Levi asked. With his back to me, his opinion of that wasn't clear, but my answer was.

"As soon as she'll have me."

He reached the end of his path, turned, and stopped. His expression was grim, but the harder I looked, the clearer it became that it was worry riding him, not resentment. I wish I could help him see that the worry for this family wasn't all on his shoulders. We shared that responsibility, but Levi wouldn't accept that. He never had.

"Bring them here, then."

I snorted. "I'd fucking love to make that happen. Just got to get Leah to agree."

Levi glanced at the ceiling, toward his own feminine half. "Good luck with that."

I thought about asking if everything was all right between the two of them, but my brother would just clam up if I did. Making a mental note to catch Abby alone tomorrow for a little interrogation, I moved into Levi's space and gave him a hard hug before slapping him on the back. "I might need it, bro. Thanks."

∞

"That's ten!" Brooke squealed as she gathered the green and red cards from the center of the table and added them to the stack in front of her.

"How can that be ten?" I protested. "How can 'kitten' win if the category is 'scary'?"

Brooke shrugged. "Ask Mommy."

"It's the crab apple version," Leah explained. On the side that Brooke couldn't see, she winked my way. "Go with it." To Brooke, "Time for bed!"

Well, if *game over* meant time for bed…

After much grumbling, Brooke was hustled into the shower. She came to find me in the kitchen when she was finished, her pink pj's with the rainbow-horned unicorns snug around her. "Remi, will you brush my hair?"

I set the last plate from dinner in the dishwasher before drying my hands on the towel tucked into my hip pocket. "You want me to brush your hair?" That didn't sound as panicked as I thought, did it? "What about Mommy?"

Leah's smirk told me the panic was loud and clear. "She wants you, big guy."

"Yeah, you, Remi. Please?"

I groaned. Who could resist that face? I was a killer, for fuck's sake. Why was it so hard to tell this child no? What if I pulled her hair? Would she cry? The thought of those blue eyes filled with tears clenched my gut in a way I'd never have admitted to six months ago.

I passed the towel to Leah. "Okay, little one, your choice."

Leah took the towel. I was a few steps away when she used it to snap my ass. "Start from the bottom."

She was laughing at me. Prowling back to her, I corralled her against the sink and gave her a quick, hard kiss. "You'll regret that later," I warned her quietly.

"I doubt it," she said, laughing out loud this time.

In the living room I sat on the floor with Brooke between my legs. "Okay, here we go." Very, very gently I brought the brush to the bottom of her long, wet blonde hair and began to work out the tangles. To my surprise, it wasn't as hard as I'd expected. Leah had explained the wonders of conditioner to me—something my brothers and I'd had no need of—but I hadn't quite believed her until now. Soon I was taking long, smooth strokes through Brooke's semidry hair as she propped her head on her arms on the table in front of her. A few minutes later, when Leah came in from the kitchen, I gathered Brooke's drooping body in my arms and carried her to her bedroom so Leah could tuck her in.

By the time Leah rejoined me in the living room, my heart had begun a hard thud that echoed in my ears.

"Come back here with me?" she asked, holding out her hand. I followed her to the "master suite," a bedroom not much bigger than Brooke's but with a full bath attached. My shoes had been kicked off earlier, and now I piled up at the head of Leah's queen-size bed, pillows at my back, to watch her change.

After stripping her T-shirt off, she unclipped her bra and slid it down her arms. "I really need to look into getting a bigger bed," she said, eyeing me.

"Why?" I asked absently, my focus on her naked skin. I knew why—because my feet hung off the end if I laid down next to her in the bed—but I didn't want her buying a new bed. I wanted her in mine.

"Because that one is too small." Tossing aside her pants, she glanced around. "Not that a king would leave much room to walk in here."

She reached for a T-shirt I was pretty sure I'd left here a couple of weeks ago. I held out my hand. "Com'ere."

Leah looked at me from under her lashes, a sly smile tugging at her lips. My gut tightened immediately. Planting her hands on the end of the bed, she began a slow crawl toward me that had my mouth going dry and needy. Round breasts dangled from her body, perfect for my hands, and that ass——

"Get up here, *lev sheli*," I demanded hoarsely.

She paused. "Why?"

I put a bit more growl into my words. "Get up here or that punishment I promised you will become reality."

She sat back on her heels.

I pounced.

The shift of Leah's laughter to soft moans as I flipped her onto her back and sucked a pink nipple into my mouth made the animal in me long to break free, but I forced him back. *Just for a few minutes.* I was already desperate to lose myself in her body, just as I had been time and again the past few weeks, but there was something else I needed so much more. And I wasn't about to let myself get distracted.

I pulled away, gliding my teeth along her nipple as I went. Leah gasped my name.

"I need to tell you something," I said, that loud thud returning to my ears. I shifted to my side next to her, intertwined our legs, and stared down, unable to believe this moment was finally here.

"Yeah?" Leah stroked her thumb along my wet lips. "Me too."

What? "What did you need to talk to me about?"

But she shook her head, eyes full of mysteries. "You first."

"All right." I guessed. Where had all the moisture in my mouth run off to? "I'm taking a job at Hacr as head of security."

"Yeah?" She shifted up onto her elbow. "Why?"

Yeah, why? "Because…" I swallowed back the drumming of my heart in my throat. How the hell did men do this? "Because I want you to move in with me, Leah. You and Brooke. I want to be everything you need me to be." I took her hand, staring at our entwined fingers, needing something, anything to focus on. "Please say yes."

She was quiet so long that I swore the silence would crush my soul. Just as I gathered a scrap of strength to get up, walk away, Leah laid back on the bed and reached up to trace the line of my jaw. Gripped the back of my neck and pulled me to her. Kissed me sweetly but thoroughly on the lips.

I started to breathe again.

"You don't have to be anyone else to be who I need," she said.

I met her deep brown eyes, so like her daughter's. A warm glow waited for me there. "I could never be good enough to deserve you."

"Wrong." She tugged her bottom lip between her teeth, worrying it for a moment. "I'm not going to lie and say this hasn't taken some getting used to, but Remi, I want you for you, not anything else. Is this job what you want?"

"Yes." Because it might give me her.

"Then congratulations." She kissed me again, lingering this time, seeming to savor the contact as much as I did. Only when we pulled back did my brain kick in and remember something important.

"Will you move in with me?"

A blush trailed across her cheeks, sweetly pink and glowing. "About that…"

I traced a finger across the soft color. "Yeah?"

"It would probably be a good idea."

I frowned at her. "Why is it a good idea? I mean, I know why I think it's a good idea, but..."

I stopped as the color in her face got brighter. "Because it's usually good for two parents to live in one place."

My frown got deeper. "What?" I was coming to love Brooke as my own, but I didn't think Leah was referring to her daughter. "I don't—"

A snort of laughter escaped her. Placing a hand on my chest, she pushed me back until she could roll on top of me. My hands went automatically to her breasts, my dick swelling as she settled above me.

"Jeremiah."

"Yeah," I said, admittedly distracted.

Leah pressed her breasts harder into my hands, humming her pleasure. "I'm pregnant."

I dropped my hands like her breasts were hot coals. A rush of air filled my ears, blocking out everything but the echo of those two words in my mind. *I'm pregnant. I'm pregnant. I'm pregnant.* "What?" I croaked.

Sitting up, Leah straddled my hips and pulled my hands up to cover her naked breasts again. Hard nipples jutted against my palms. "I'm pregnant, Remi."

"Holy shit." What the hell had happened to my lungs? Why couldn't I get air?

I swear I blacked out, something I doubted Leah would ever let me forget. And if my brothers found out? But fucking A, a baby? A— Jesus.

I wasn't sure how I got there, but the next thing I knew, I was on all fours over Leah's body, my gaze riveted on her belly. "Are you sure?"

Her hands stroked softly over my shoulders, and I had the feeling she was trying to calm me before I had a heart attack. *Too fucking late for that.*

"I'm sure."

I'm sure. I closed my eyes, letting the word sink deep into my heart, into that place where only Leah had ever entered.

A baby.

I opened my eyes. My clothes went flying.

"Remi!" Leah was giggling, scooting back from the frenzy. I yanked the last sock off my foot, scrambled after her, and was tucking my hard cock into her body before she had time to get away.

"Oh!"

She arched back, her legs opening to let me in, her breasts bouncing as I entered her. The most beautiful sight I'd ever seen. The sexiest woman I'd ever known—and she was carrying my baby.

"This is going to be fast, *lev sheli*," I growled.

"Yes. Fast." Leah's smile could light up the world. "Take me, Jeremiah."

I did.

∞

Ella Sheridan

Did you enjoy Assassin's Heart? If so, you can leave a
review at your favorite retailer to tell other readers
about the book. And thank you!

Don't miss the exciting extras from the ASSASSINS
series, available only through my newsletter.
Sign up at ellasheridanauthor.com.

∞

Before you go…

You met King and Charlotte in ASSASSIN'S
HEART. Now read their story.

DENY ME

Southern Nights: Enigma 4

King Moncrief walked away from a life of privilege
and wealth—and the woman he loved—to answer the
call to serve, first as a cop, then as a security specialist
for JCL Securities. Helping is in his blood, but it can't
keep him warm at night. Not when dreams of what

could have been, what will never be, leave him cold to the core.

Charlotte Alexander lost the two most important things in her life just out of high school: her childhood sweetheart and her only chance at having a child. Now her energy is poured into the charity she founded, Creating Families, helping low-income couples achieve their dream of adopting. But something isn't right at CF, and when Charlotte is targeted by a killer, there's only one place to turn.

Back to the past. To the man who walked away. The man she denied but never forgot.

∞

Chapter One

The trailer park was definitely on the wrong side of the tracks, but Charlotte Alexander had never cared. She'd been here numerous times—to pick Becky up for appointments, drop her off afterward, to bring groceries or paperwork or supplies she'd stocked for the baby's arrival. Three weeks. That's how close they were to delivery. The couple planning to adopt Becky's baby were ecstatic.

Tomorrow they'd be heartbroken.

This afternoon the dilapidated state of the white and rust trailer served to remind Charlotte of everything that was at stake, not just for the baby but for Becky. She parked her car in the patchy grass in front of the girl's home, her gaze falling on shiny chrome and slick paint. A motorcycle gleamed in the weak sunlight filtering through the pines overhead. A very expensive motorcycle. She didn't know enough about brands to identify it, but the sheer power in its body screamed money. Something Becky and her family didn't have.

Or shouldn't.

Her belly twisted as she stared at the machine, beautiful in comparison to the old pickup next to it, the neglected home beside it. Only one person in that trailer could drive a bike that size—Becky's father, Richard Jones. Big and mean, he'd intimidated Charlotte from the get-go, but because she was helping get Becky's baby "out of my goddamn house," as he put it, Richard had kept his distance. Today might not go as well, but intimidated or not, Charlotte needed answers. Needed to make sure Becky and the baby were all right.

Taking a deep breath for courage, she pushed open her car door on the exhale and stepped out. Her heel sank into the red clay soil as she put her weight on it. There'd been no time to change after the late lunch she'd hosted with potential contributors earlier, and she was highly conscious of the luxury inherent in her dress clothes as she crossed the stubby grass toward rickety wooden stairs leading to the front door. Her usual daily uniform—dress slacks and button-downs—worked for the office and interacting with both less fortunate girls and couples from all walks of life, but schmoozing those in her social circle for funding was a fact of life she'd accepted long ago. And moneyed contributors preferred moneyed directors; hence, the fancy clothes.

Right now, though, the same clothes that helped draw large donations underscored the vast ravine between her life and sixteen-year-old Becky's, something she never wanted to rub in the girl's face. Today she had no choice.

The rail wobbled as she grabbed it on the first step up the stairs. When her foot landed on the second step, the sound of the chain lock sliding reached her ears. She paused in her climb.

The door cracked open a few inches. Becky's features were pinched as she peered out of the narrow opening. "What are you doing here?"

The whispered words carried the rasp of fear. Anxiety was etched into the dark circles under her tired eyes, and a faint purple bruise marred her cheekbone.

"Becky, hon..." Instinctively her hand rose, needing to touch the girl, to reassure her. To yank her from the trailer and carry her far away where she'd never have to worry about being hit again. "Are you okay?"

"You shouldn't be here, Charlotte." Tears welled, but Becky sniffed them away. "You need to go. Now."

"Come with me."

The door opened a few more inches, allowing the swell of Becky's belly to push through. Charlotte had walked beside the girl every step of the way after she'd come to Creating Families to talk about giving her child up for adoption. She'd watched that mound go from a tiny swell to a basketball. Taking a personal interest in the women who came to her organization was a point of pride with Charlotte. They didn't only care for the babies they helped adopt—caring for the mothers, during and long after their pregnancies, helping them build new lives for themselves, was a hallmark of Creating Families' work. But she'd always had a special place in her heart for Becky, maybe because the girl reminded her of herself at that age. Of what might have been had the love of her life not walked away without a backward glance.

Had her body not betrayed her.

Shoving the memories away, she gripped the railing hard enough that a splinter sank beneath her skin. "Becky, please. Come with me. He can't force you—"

"Yes, he can." A wary glance over her shoulder told Charlotte exactly why Becky was whispering. "I know why you're here. I know you don't understand why I'd back out of the adoption. Trust me, if I had any choice, I wouldn't. But I—"

"Who you talking to?"

The barked question sent a jolt through Becky's body. Her eyes went wide, her grip tightening on the door just before it was torn from her hand. Richard towered behind her, his unshaven face and stained white tank so cliché Charlotte would've laughed if she wasn't so busy trying not to reveal a hint of fear. The man's mean eyes narrowed on her, turning her knees to water.

"Why you here, rich bitch?"

Speak, Charlotte. Becky needs you.

"I came to check on Becky."

A heavy palm landed on Becky's thin shoulder. The girl jumped. "Nothing for you to check on here, lady." The man sneered. "We don't need your charity no more."

How had such a sweet girl come from this asshole?

"Becky doesn't—"

"That's right, she don't. Her bastard don't either. She don't have to go through with no adoption. Now get out of here before I make sure you regret bothering us."

She glanced toward Becky, whose face had gone sheet-white. Worry for the girl kept Charlotte in place. "Sir, I just want—"

A growl tore from the man's mouth as he shoved Becky aside. "Get off my property, bitch!"

His bulk pushing onto the stairs caused Charlotte to teeter backward. One heel slipped from the step. For a second she thought she could pull herself back upright, and then she was falling through the air, her stomach lurching at the loss of equilibrium. Pain slammed into her as her butt landed on the concrete pad below the stairs.

Becky's father huffed a laugh. Staring down his nose, he hocked out a glob of spit that landed perilously close to her hand. "Remember what I said. Come back and I'll make you regret it. Becky ain't your concern no more."

The door slammed behind him, the slide of the chain lock being repositioned reaching her ears past the ringing that filled them. It took a minute before she could gather herself enough to struggle to her feet, seconds when she searched the windows of the trailer in hopes of seeing Becky's face, making some kind of connection with the girl she'd grown so close to, but no face appeared. No sound came. Nothing.

She stood, dusting red clay from her backside with hands that shook like leaves, uncertain what to do. Whatever it was, she couldn't do it alone. "I'll be back, hon. I promise," she said, knowing Becky couldn't hear her but desperate to let the girl know. It felt like a betrayal to walk back to her car, slide behind the wheel, but what choice did she have?

David hadn't defeated Goliath empty-handed. Her only choice was to find her stones and return to battle. That didn't make it easier to back the car away from the trailer and drive away. She didn't feel like David; she felt like a monster, leaving the victim with her abuser.

Without conscious thought, without a decision on her part, she pointed the car toward home, but when she reached the turnoff, she kept going. That same mindlessness took her miles down the road, south of town, past Lake McIntosh. Toward the piece of land that, no matter how lush with trees and hills, no matter how soothing the rocky creek that wound through its heart, shouldn't be a balm. It should be a reminder of all she'd lost because of her own foolishness.

Too bad it was the only place she felt truly safe.

The canopy enveloped her car in hushed shadows as she nosed her way onto the dirt road, the only access to the property. That was all it took for the hard shell she'd surrounded herself with back at the trailer to crack.

Why are you doing this? You know you shouldn't be here.

And yet here was the only place she could just *be*, where she could let the shaking overtake her and cry the tears choking the back of her throat and give in to the fear shuddering through her in soul-sucking waves. Here, where no one could see. Where no one knew how weak she really was.

Where she could pretend that the arms that used to hold her safe, right here in this very spot, were still around her.

It was stupid. Senseless. That didn't stop it from being true. The sobs came, shook her down to her bones. She sobbed until her stomach turned to stone and everything inside it threatened to come back up. Her chest went tight as a drum and she had a hard time breathing, but she let herself ride the waves until, finally, the stress subsided.

Long minutes later the muffled ring of her phone pulled her back to reality. Scrambling in her purse, she felt the cool rectangle of her cell all the way at the bottom and pulled it out. A glance at the screen brought a groan to her lips.

She tapped the green circle. "Mom."

The word wasn't as bright and cheery as she'd like, but hopefully it was close enough to fool her mother. Both her parents were supportive of her charity work, and at twenty-eight they recognized the futility of convincing her to do anything else, but if they knew someone had threatened her? All bets would be off.

"What's wrong?"

Thank God her mom couldn't see the grimace that twisted her mouth. "Why would anything be wrong?"

"Don't try that 'answering a question with a question' bit, young lady." Kim Alexander might have been born and bred into the highest tier of Southern society, but she was also a hands-on mother who knew her daughter well, right down to the nuances of her voice. Damn it.

Leaning her head back on the headrest, Charlotte let a heavy sigh escape her, taking the last of her tears with it. The tension in her belly stayed behind. "Just some things going on at work, Mom. Really."

"Did the luncheon go well today?"

Creating Families had gained generous donations this afternoon, no doubt about it. But it was what they'd lost, what Becky had lost, that consumed her.

"Very well." She cranked her car, another sigh escaping her when the cool air from the vent hit her heated face. "I'm just about to head home." It was early for her, but today had been far longer than the actual hours she'd put in.

A long silence on her mother's end didn't bode well for her chances of ending the interrogation. Then, "I'll make some tea; how does that sound?"

Tea cured a multitude of ills, according to Kim Alexander. "Make mine iced and you got it. I'll be there in a little bit."

"Sacrilege!" A smile flavored her mom's words. Delicate laughter filtered through the line, curving Charlotte's lips despite her worries. "I'll make it anyway. Be careful, hon."

Careful. She glanced at the beauty before her. She needed to be careful with more than just driving.

Packing her emotions and her memories away, she put the car in reverse. Headed toward the highway and home. But with every mile, Becky's situation nagged at her. The pain in the girl's eyes. The bruise on her cheek. There had to be something she could do.

First things first. Time for a legal opinion. Hitting speed-dial on her console, she waited for the phone to ring.

"You've reached Wes Moncrief. I'm away at the moment. Please leave a message so I can return your call."

Beep.

"Hey, Wes. It's Charlotte." She didn't have to identify herself—they'd known each other practically since birth, which was part of why he was her closest friend—but she did anyway. Always. Because…

She pushed that thought away.

"Listen, I was hoping I could talk to you about something going on with one of the girls. I just…I don't know." She paused to round a curve, trying to bring her words together and failing. Chewed the inside of her lip. "I need some help."

Accelerating through the bend in the road, she eyed the short straightaway ahead. Could Wes help? He served as part of the legal team for Creating Families, but Becky had already terminated her agreement. What could he do?

Ask that question when you talk to him.

For now she said, "The situation's complicated, but I'm hoping…" What? She slowed for the next curve. "I don't know. We'll talk later. Will I see you at—"

A flash at the corner of her eye had her jerking her head around.

A pickup truck, its grill massive to her eyes, barreled toward her from a side road. There was no time to get out of the way. There wasn't even time to scream. One second she was staring down that grill; the next, everything went black.

Chapter Two

A huge yawn crept over King Moncrief before he could hold it back. The sound of his jaw popping was loud in his ears.

"Look at that yawn," Saint, his best friend, crowed. "Only one thing makes you that tired, right, buddy?"

"Jet lag?" Elliot asked, tossing the files she carried onto the conference table. Since King had returned from an off-the-record assignment in Ireland just yesterday, it was a reasonable—and much more likely than what Saint was thinking—guess.

"No," Saint growled.

Elliot chuckled, the sound rich with amused condescension.

King's laugh was more subdued. Jet lag was definitely kicking his ass this morning. Saint knew him far too well to think he'd been out partying, but that didn't stop the prick from giving him a hard time.

Work had provided all the excitement they needed lately, just not the good kind. Dain, their team lead, had almost lost his wife to a workplace hostage situation; Elliot's rapist/slaver father had tracked her down and almost killed her; and just last week, a close friend of their team, Fionn McCullough, had needed help in Ireland to protect his mother from the head of an Irish cartel.

Hopefully things would slow down now. They could do their jobs for JCL Securities, relax on their off days, and get back to some sense of normal. At least until Dain and Olivia's baby was born, but that was closer to Christmas, nearly two months away.

The door to the conference room opened, and Dain walked in. "Morning." He strode to the head of the table, a cup of coffee in his hand, his thick black Mohawk spiking the air like he'd jammed his fingers through it on the way here. "We've got some cleanup on a couple of cases that we need to get to work on—"

Groans circled the table. Cleanup was code for paperwork, and no one wanted to do paperwork.

Dain flashed a sadistic grin. "Stop whining, babies."

Saint fake cried. Elliot knocked him upside the back of the head.

"King, you're excused."

King straightened, grimacing as tension pulled at his fatigued muscles. Jet lag really was a bitch. "What did I do?"

"Nothing. You have a visitor." His boss settled in the chair at the head of the table and opened the laptop he'd been carrying. "There's nothing urgent going on right now that we can't handle, so head on over and see what he wants. He's waiting for you at Lori's desk."

"Why didn't she call me?" And who the hell was visiting him on a Monday at seven thirty in the morning?

"'Cause I was passing by at just the right time." Dain's dark eyes fixed on him, the lack of tension there telling him the work they had this week truly wasn't pressing. King pulled his weight, always. More than his weight if his team would let him, which they didn't most of the time. They were all alphas, Elliot included, and none of them let themselves slack off.

Even Saint, no matter how laid-back and easygoing he seemed.

"All right." Instead of wasting time asking more questions, he nodded at his teammates, flipped Saint a bird while Dain was distracted by his computer, then took himself and his coffee out the conference room door.

JCL Securities had made a name for itself from the day the business opened. Conlan James and Jack Quinn, the owners, were already well-known in the local security community before they'd gone into business together. Now, just eight years later, they were the premier security company in the US. King had joined them, and Dain's team, after several years with the Atlanta PD, and he hadn't looked back. The hands-on approach to keeping people safe, to saving lives, was all he'd hoped for when he'd left home a decade ago.

Service was in his heart, even if it wasn't in his blood. It was his passion. He didn't think he was capable of feeling for a woman what he felt for his work. Not anymore.

The front office of JCL was painted a cool, serene blue, the corner taken up by a trickling fountain that calmed the nerves of those who waited here. Lori Jordan, the front receptionist, had been with the company from the get-go. She ruled the office with an iron fist gloved in Southern sweetness that could charm the gruffest, snootiest clients. This morning she matched the room in a pale blue dress that flowed down her arms and fluttered across her collarbone.

"Morning, Miss Lori." He wasn't sure why he called her *miss*. It just seemed to fit, had since the day he'd met her. "A Mohawked bird told me someone was here to see me?"

"More like a falcon." Lori grinned. "A big one. That man has predator written all over him."

A laugh lifted his fatigue the slightest bit. "No argument here."

"You do have a visitor." Lori nodded toward the corner. "A Mr. Wes Moncrief. I'm assuming you're related?"

King heard her words, the name, but at the edge of his hearing where gray haze was taking over. All his focus had zeroed in on the tall man in a ten-thousand-dollar suit sitting near the fountain. His body was tense, his elbows on his knees, the fingers laced together in front of his face white where he squeezed them.

Wes. His first cousin. The cousin he hadn't seen in a decade.

The reason for that gap pounded at his brain, threatening his control. King tightened the straps on the memories as he strode across the room.

"Is it Mom and Dad?" he asked. Wes's body language screamed disaster, and there was only one reason his first cousin would be here, now, in his office, looking like that.

Wes's blond head popped up, his gaze, a few shades darker than King's own light blue, grabbing on to his like a lifeline. "What?"

King pulled Wes to his feet, absently noting that his cousin had filled out in the years they'd been apart. He'd grown into a man from the high school kid he'd been back then. And King had missed it. Grief creeped along the edges of his mind. "Mom and Dad. Did something happen to them?"

"No." Wes shook his head, the vee between his brows deepening. "No, I'm here about Charlotte."

All the breath left King's lungs at the sound of her name. The straps keeping his past in check broke with a sharp snap, a million memories, sensations, emotions hitting him at once. Things he'd tried hard to forget. Things he'd never been able to completely erase. "Is she all right?"

God, please let her be all right.

"She's—" Wes shoved a hand through his already mussed hair. "She's all right. For now." Glancing around the room, he lowered his voice. "Can we talk in private?"

"Of course. This way."

His answer sounded so calm, like he didn't want to shake his cousin until the answers to all his questions were forced through his rattling teeth. But no, he was King Moncrief. He was logical, in control. Cold, some people said.

He felt anything but cold right now.

The drumbeat of their steps echoed threateningly as they walked down the hall. They passed the conference room where his team was meeting, and he caught Saint's glance up, his gaze following them. Farther down the hall, he opened the door to a smallish room with a window, the desk in the middle taking up most of the space. "Have a seat."

Wes took the armchair in front of the desk, while King settled behind it. He'd left for Ireland in a rush last week, and the evidence of his hurry lay in the chaos on his normally neat desk. He ignored it, zeroing in on Wes. "Tell me."

Worry clouded his cousin's eyes. "Someone tried to kill Charlotte."

If Wes had punched him in the gut, he couldn't have been more surprised, but he kept the reaction locked behind a facade of calm along with everything else roiling inside him. "Why do you think that?"

"I don't know why." He rubbed at his eyes. "At least, I'm not sure—"

King held up a hand. "What do the police say?"

"Random accident." Wes's mouth tightened. "It wasn't an accident. I don't know why they won't believe her, but I know it wasn't."

If they were dealing with the smallish station near his old neighborhood, the cops there played a lot of politics. Peachtree City was the wealthiest suburb of Atlanta, and serious crimes rarely occurred there. Knowing one had could hurt the city's reputation.

The work part of King's brain, the logical part of him, clicked on. This was Charlotte they were discussing, but he couldn't think about that right now. He leaned forward over his desk. "Okay, start from the beginning. What happened?"

"She was coming home from work yesterday." He glanced out the window for a second, his profile so like King's that the familiarity gripped his heart, squeezing tight. He hadn't seen a face that familiar in so long. "She was almost home when a truck smashed into her from a side street. T-boned her. On her side of the car."

King sucked in his breath. He knew those roads. Wes had said Charlotte was all right, which meant she'd been incredibly lucky. A direct hit could've tumbled her down a steep hillside or, even worse, killed her instantly.

She could be dead. His Charlotte. *Dead.* He squeezed his hands into fists below the edge of the desk.

"She went over the railing"—King's heart stopped—"but slammed into a tree a few feet down, keeping her from too far of a fall," Wes said. "Luckily her car has direct assistance. The company called police as soon as the accident registered on their system."

Thank God for expensive perks. He didn't want to imagine her, hurt and alone, scrambling for a cell that could've been who knew where.

"Did whoever hit her stop?"

"No." Wes's eyes narrowed. "The police can't find them. They think the guy ran because he didn't want to be arrested, but…"

"But what?"

That blond head shook. Blue eyes bored into his. "She'd just been to visit a client. She told the police the father threatened her."

"You think he could've had something to do with this." It seemed a bit too obvious, and smart criminals usually avoided the obvious if they could. But King knew better than most that not all criminals were smart.

Desperation deepened the lines on Wes's face. King couldn't miss the intensity of emotion there, the fact that his cousin's body practically shook with the need to do something. This wasn't mere worry over a friend of the family. No, it was something much, much more.

He forced himself to tuck that thought away as well.

"That area has a clear line of sight. Whoever hit her knew she was coming. Where the road curves around the McAllister estate, with that reinforced guardrail? She was slammed into it, crushed between it and the truck before it gave way.

"The only evidence left behind was some paint scrapings and the rusted grill. A Chevy pickup, heavy duty, it looks like. They're 'looking into it,'"—Wes made air quotes—"but my friends at the station say they're just blowing us off to keep us quiet."

A work truck like he was describing was common in rural Georgia, but not in the exclusive area near Charlotte's family home. Especially not a rusted one. "No one saw anything?"

"No. She was left there, alone, for around five minutes before the ambulance arrived."

Anxiety tightened his muscles. Charlotte helpless, bleeding, hurting. All the discipline he'd learned as a cop, as a security specialist—hell, all the discipline in the world couldn't keep him from picturing it. From needing to get to her. Keep her safe.

It bothered Wes just as much; anger and pain dripped from his words.

"Wes…why did you come to me?"

"Because if anyone can figure out what's going on, it's you." Wes stood, turned to pace, then sat again. "What if the guy comes back? What if I'm right and it wasn't an accident and he tries something else?"

"The cops—"

"Don't want to rock the boat hard enough to have an attempted murder become public knowledge!" Wes stopped, took a breath, obviously struggling to get himself back under control. "Her parents are too shaken to even realize the cops are just shuffling around papers. Charlotte needs someone who doesn't care about reputation, and we both know you're the perfect man for that job."

King ignored the jab. "Even if there is more going on here than what they say, Charlotte is not going to want me involved."

"King…" Wes leaned forward, his intensity pinning King to his seat. "I haven't asked anything of you, ever. I supported you even when your parents cut you off. I gave you the distance you obviously wanted. But I'm asking you now, please, to help me keep her safe. Just…ask some questions. Investigate. If you say there's nothing suspicious, well then…" He spread his hands. "You're the only person I know to ask. The only person I know who can do this."

The desperation in his cousin's face couldn't be ignored. Wes needed him—to protect Charlotte, the woman he'd walked away from a decade ago. The woman Wes obviously had strong feelings for, maybe even loved.

Could he do it? Could he walk back into her life?

He thought hard about the answer to that question. She might not welcome him or accept his help. And if she didn't care, if she returned Wes's feelings? He ignored the way his gut clenched at the thought. What mattered was her safety and Wes's request, not his own feelings.

Finally he nodded. "I can't promise anything, but I'll come out and talk to her."

Wes stood, reaching for King's hand as he came to his feet as well. "That's all I can ask. I appreciate it."

King rounded the desk to pull Wes into a hug. "I know. I hope I can help." He held his cousin a bit longer than he normally would, savoring the contact with his own flesh and blood. "I missed you, man." And he had, more than he'd realized.

Wes drew back slowly, giving him a worry-tinged smile. "You too."

"Let me talk to my team lead and I'll let you know when I can be there."

"As soon as possible," Wes insisted. "I'll go with you."

Chapter Three

"Wes is meeting us at the house," her mother said as she helped Charlotte settle into the wheelchair the nurse had pushed into the room. Charlotte ducked her head, hiding her expression. The topic of Wes was one she wasn't up to discussing, not right now. She was too battered, physically and emotionally. There wasn't a muscle in her body that didn't hurt, but that was nothing compared to the fear crouching at the back of her mind.

"Such a good man," Dale Alexander said from his position holding the door open. "When are you going to put him out of his misery and say—"

Charlotte raised her hand, noting that it shook the slightest bit. "Not now, Dad. Okay?" It was a common conversation, but not one she could deal with in her hospital room after coming too close to dying.

Her father's sharp features softened. Coming to kneel in front of the wheelchair, he laid a big hand over both her knees. "Of course." He squeezed slightly. "Let's get you home. That's the important thing."

A rush of affection and sheer gratitude that she hadn't lost them filled her a bit too full. "Right." His stubbled cheek tickled her lips when she kissed it, just like it had since she was a child. "Let's go home."

She closed her eyes on the ride back to the house, not wanting to see the spot where her accident had occurred. She'd woken up multiple times last night, her heart in her throat, her body rigid with panic, always with that image of the truck grill filling her mind. The nightmare seemed to play on a loop in her subconscious. Between it and the constant nurse checks to see if her concussion was worsening, she'd barely rested, much less slept. All she wanted was a shower and her bed—and maybe one of the pain pills the doctor had sent home with her. If it would keep her sleeping deep enough not to dream, she'd take it.

The slowing of the car outside the gates of the house registered, the familiar creak of the wires as they drew the heavy wrought-iron panels back. The sound had signaled *home* since she was a little girl. Now they signaled safety, and her muscles went slack with relief and fatigue.

"Almost there," her mom said beside her, almost as if she sensed Charlotte's response.

She opened her eyes, her gaze sweeping the wooded lawn until it snagged on the front door. Two cars, one Wes's silver Mercedes, the other a sleek electric-blue sports car she'd never seen before, waited in the circular drive. Her father passed them to stop at the bottom of the steps leading to the front entrance. "Wait there," he said. "I'll carry you inside."

The snort that escaped her made her head hurt. She rubbed at it gently. "You're not carrying me inside, Dad." But he was already out the door and coming around. "Tell him he's not carrying me, Mom."

Her mother patted her hand. "We almost lost you. If carrying you makes him feel better, let him."

Which was how she found herself entering the foyer in her father's arms. When he turned toward the sitting room, she protested again, knowing it was as futile as the first time. "I'm really not up to company." She wanted her room and her bed. Why was that so hard to get?

"Wes isn't company," her dad grumbled in her ear. "You need some food in you before you take any medicine. Let him see you, just for a few minutes."

He'd always been Team Wes. She couldn't make him see that Wes was a friend, not husband material. No one was, not for her. Not after——

"Charlotte!"

She glanced in Wes's direction to see him hurrying toward her, worry lining his handsome face. "I'm fine, really. I can walk. Dad wouldn't let me."

"I seconded the motion," her mother said, trailing them into the room. "It's not every day we get to baby you..." The last word trailed off, only to be followed by a sharp, "What are you doing here?"

Charlotte glanced at her mother, who stared somewhere across the room. Her dad settled her on the long couch, blocking her view. "What is it?"

Wes sat at her feet and pulled her shoes off without asking, and she caught a glimpse of what she swore was guilt in his eyes. Guilt over what?

Dale Alexander straightened, turned, and a rough growl left his throat. "What—"

"I asked him to come," Wes said.

"Asked who?" Who in the world could make her parents react this way?

The *who* stepped into her line of sight, just beyond Wes. A sharp gasp choked her. Of course. Only one man could decimate her parents' manners, and that man was standing in their sitting room.

Kingsley Moncrief.

For a minute the sense of unreality blocked out everything else. The room spun, and she worried she might faint. It was too much on top of everything else—the fight at Becky's, the wreck, almost dying, her parents, and now... "King."

His face was inscrutable, those eerily light blue eyes blank, revealing nothing. "Charlotte." He nodded toward her. "I trust you really are fine. What did the doctor say?"

"What business is it of yours, Moncrief?" her father demanded.

"I asked him to come," Wes said again. The why was what escaped her.

Her parents too, obviously. The tension in both their bodies screamed anger, but it was her mother's mottled face, the glint of tears burning in her eyes that hurt Charlotte the most. Wes might've meant well, but...

"I don't think—"

Wes cut her off. "I've spoken with the police."

Her father's hands tightened into fists as he angled himself to face off with Wes, cutting King out of the discussion. "And?"

Wes shoved a hand through his thick blond hair. "And despite what they might have assured you, Dale, they aren't going to pursue this very hard."

She would've doubted his words, but Wes could get behind the official reports to the truth. She and her parents couldn't.

Where did that leave them?

The cry that left her mother ripped through Charlotte's head. "It wasn't an accident! Why is that obvious to everyone but them?"

"You know why," Wes said. "A possible attempted murder, here in Peachtree City?"

"That would tarnish the city's reputation," her father said, the rough edges of the words showing exactly how he felt about the idea.

"That doesn't explain why *he* is here."

Her mother had managed to ask the question Charlotte found impossible to voice. She swore she saw a wince in King's expression before he turned his attention to her parents.

Wes squared his shoulders, determination in the lines of his body. "I've asked King to help us investigate."

Her mother rounded the couch to sit at Charlotte's feet, placing a protective hand over her chilled flesh. The hand gripped her firmly, steadied her. "How could he help us? It's ludicrous."

They didn't know who King was now. Not that Charlotte would tell them. That would mean revealing her secret: that she'd never stopped following his career, following him. She understood exactly why Wes had gone to his cousin, despite their history.

More history than King or even Wes knew.

King cleared his throat. "I work for JCL Securities now."

Her parents exchanged a glance. JCL was a renowned firm, one of Atlanta's pride-and-joy corporations. Anyone who was anyone in the city knew the owners, Conlan James and Jack Quinn, by reputation if not in person.

In the silence following his words, Charlotte peeked from beneath her lashes toward King, let herself examine the man who'd left her behind ten years ago. To take him in. He'd aged, no longer the fresh-from-college young man she'd loved back then. Unfortunately for her, the years only added to his appeal. Still tall, he'd filled out, muscles riding the expanse of his shoulders, broadening his chest. Even through the button-down shirt and sport coat he wore, she could tell he was strong, fit. The tension of leashed energy added to his aura of capability, leaving no doubt that he could handle himself in a fight. He was more bad boy than tender lover now.

Lines gave character to his face instead of taking it away, the edge of his jaw and cheekbones somehow harder than before. Or maybe time had made her forget. She couldn't forget those lips, though, soft when he wanted, hard when he needed them to be. And those eyes, the ones that used to see into her soul...

His penetrating stare met hers through the crowd between them, sending a stroke of lightning down her spine. Taking her breath. Stopping her heart. Dredging up emotions that threatened to push her over the edge of control.

Her mother felt the jolt and glanced at her, a frown deepening the vee between her perfect brows. "I don't think—"

Her father held up a hand, forestalling her mother's protest.

"Dale, you can't possibly be considering this," Kim Alexander said.

A wealth of emotion that had nothing to do with Charlotte's accident filled the words. And based on the roller coaster the few minutes in the same room with him had generated, Charlotte agreed. She didn't need this right now.

But who else could help? Not just her, but Becky.

Guilt that she hadn't considered the girl till now swamped her. "Mom—"

"What's your plan?" her father asked.

"For now," King said, "nothing official." His glance skipped off Charlotte's quickly. "I'd like to get more details, and then a friend and I can go check out the guy Charlotte met with."

"Becky's still there," she said. "She's alone with him. If he did this to me, what..." But she couldn't force the question out. What had happened to her in the time Charlotte had been in the hospital?

This time King's gaze latched on to hers. "I won't leave until I make absolutely certain she's okay."

The promise eased the tight knot in her stomach. She shouldn't trust any promise from him, she knew that—he'd promised her forever, after all—but here, now...what choice did she have? "Okay."

Her mother's protests scraped along her nerves, making her remember exactly how much her body hurt, how much her brain just wanted to shut down and forget about all of this. She wanted escape so badly she could barely stand to sit here and not scream. But Becky didn't have an escape. The girl needed her.

"Mom." Charlotte let her fatigue peek through. "Would you get me something to eat? I really need that pain medicine."

The request did what a hundred arguments couldn't do, kick-started that mothering instinct. Her mother's lips tightened. After a sharp glance in King's direction, as if to assure herself he wasn't coming any closer to her precious daughter, she stood. "I'll be right back."

One down, one to go. Although she thought her dad was already halfway to agreeing. When he took her mom's place on the couch and circled her ankle with a warm hand, she felt something settle inside her. Taking a deep breath, she forced herself to meet King's gaze head-on.

"What do you need to know?"

∞

"Ms. Sheridan writes suspense that grabs you and

won't let go."

~ Tea and Book

About The Author

Ella Sheridan never fails to take her readers to the dark edges of love and back again. Strong heroines are her signature, and her heroes span the gamut from hot rock stars to alpha bodyguards and everywhere in between. Ella never pulls her punches, and her unique combination of raw emotion, hot sex, and action leave her readers panting for the next release.

Born and raised in the Deep South, Ella writes romantic suspense, erotic romance, and hot BDSM contemporaries. Start anywhere—every book may be read as a standalone, or begin with book one in any series and watch the ties between the characters grow.

Connect with Ella at:

Ella's Website – ellasheridanauthor.com
Facebook – Ella Sheridan: Books and News
Twitter – @AuthorESheridan
Instagram – @AuthorESheridan
Pinterest – @AuthorESheridan
Bookbub – Ella Sheridan
E-mail – ella@ellasheridanauthor.com

For news on Ella's new releases, free book opportunities, and more, sign up for Ella's newsletter on her website. Or join Ella's Escape Room on Facebook for daily fun, games, and first dibs on all the news!

Made in the USA
Monee, IL
07 November 2022

17276425R00156